Th… rs

Michael Cunningham is the author of three other novels: *Golden States*, *A Home at the End of the World* and *Flesh and Blood*. *The Hours* was awarded both the 1999 Pulitzer Prize for Fiction and the 1999 Pen/Faulkner Award.

Praise for *The Hours* ~

'*The Hours* refracts the lives of three women through the prism of a single day. Michael Cunningham evokes these three discrete characters with rare skill. Their lives resonate with association as the author explores ideas of duty, sexuality, aesthetic creativity, the fluid boundaries of physical and mental health and the ultimate solution of suicide. His prose evokes nuances of atmosphere and impulse that affect each character's capacity to be satisfied with the world whether it is Virginia tentatively blocking out the new novel, Clarissa's easily shattered delicacy as she negotiates the robustness of New York, or Laura assessing the imperfections of her amateurish cake.

The references to Woolf's life and writing in *The Hours* are numerous and sophisticated, and Cunningham's gently intellectual prose would stand dissection by lovers of her work. His publisher claims that knowledge of *Mrs Dalloway* is not prerequisite, but I feel – and feeling is the operative medium of *The Hours* – that the novel would be lacking without it. And so, with a nervous nod to the lunatic narrator of Nabokov's *Pale Fire*, I suggest you read Cunningham's eloquent novel, read *Mrs Dalloway*, and then slip back into quiet enjoyment of this flattering homage to Virginia Woolf.' *Financial Times*

'Engrossing, imaginative and humane.' *Observer*

'This chamber piece rhapsodises on creativity and madness, love and loss.' *Esquire*

'The concept behind the novel is bold, the execution rich with feeling. Cunningham's engagement with *Mrs Dalloway* is a living thing; closely as his novel shadows and echoes Woolf's, it does not seem derivative. Its central premise is proved: *Mrs Dalloway* is such a powerful creation that it can be entered and reimagined in different ways.' Helen Dunmore, *The Times*

'Michael Cunningham's new novel may have been inspired by Virginia Woolf's *Mrs Dalloway* – working title: "The Hours" – but it quickly slips free of these moorings to become a far more daring, imaginative project than might be implied by the idea of an updated "classic". And for all its parallels with Woolf's novel, and its shared preoccupation with the consonance and dissonance between organised society and the chaotic life of the interior, it successfully establishes itself as its own novel, with a distinctive sensibility, cast of characters and story, or stories, to tell.' *Guardian*

'*The Hours* is little more than 200 pages long, and one can't help marvelling at the economy of Cunningham's prose which allows the development and suggestion of many pertinent themes. The book is like an echo-chamber in which the references from the original *Mrs Dalloway* connect with the latter-day stories and then seem to take on a life of their own.' Mark Bostridge, *Independent on Sunday*

'*The Hours* has the grace of a ballet: the characters shimmer and quest, each in a specific section of fractured time. It is a prism. Through the narrative, with its assortment of intense stories, the author makes a persuasive exploration of time, love, loyalties and creativity. Cunningham is operating at such a high level of art that the connections are invisible; more importantly, the coincidences are subtle, surprising and powerful. It is unusual for a novelist to say so much so economically. Although this novel does not depend on contacts and connections, such is the quality of the prose that he can draw upon shocks and revelations with the assurance of a thriller writer.' *Irish Times*

Praise for *The Hours* in America ~

'A set of contemporary characters re-voices the patterns of Virginia Woolf's *Mrs Dalloway*. It is not a pastiche but a transplanting: an exquisitely written, kaleidoscopic work that anchors a floating post-modern world on pre-modern caissons of love, grief and transcendent longing.' *Los Angeles Times*

'Cunningham's emulation of such a revered writer as Woolf is courageous, and this is his most mature and masterful work.' *Washington Post*

'We don't have to have read *Mrs Dalloway* before we can read *The Hours* and no amount of pedantic, comparison-hunting will help us understand it if we don't understand it already. But the connections between the two books . . . are so rich and subtle and offbeat that not to read *Mrs Dalloway* after we've read *The Hours* seems like a horrible denial of a readily available pleasure – as if we were to leave a concert just when the variations were getting interesting.' *New York Times*

Also by Michael Cunningham

Golden States (1984)
A Home at the End of the World (1990)
Flesh and Blood (1995)

The Hours

MICHAEL CUNNINGHAM

TED SMART

This edition produced for The Book People Ltd,
Hall Wood Avenue, Haydock, St Helens WA11 9UL

This paperback edition published in 1999
First published in Great Britain in 1999 by
Fourth Estate
A Division of HarperCollins*Publishers*
77-85 Fulham Palace Road
London W6 8JB
www.4thestate.com

Portions of this book have appeared in somewhat different form in
The New Yorker

Extracts from *Mrs. Dalloway* by Virginia Woolf; permission kindly granted by The Society of Authors as the Literary Representative of the Estate of Virginia Woolf.
Extracts from *The Diary of Virginia Woolf*, vol. 2, 1920–24, edited by Anne Olivier Bell; permission kindly granted by The Hogarth Press, Random House.
Extracts from *The Letters of Virginia Woolf*, vol. 5, 1936–1941, edited by Nigel Nicholson; permission kindly granted by The Hogarth Press, Random House.

8 9 10

A catalogue record for this book is available from the British Library.

ISBN 0 00766 659 4

Printed in Great Britain by
Clays Ltd, St Ives plc

This book is for Ken Corbett

We'll hunt for a third tiger now, but like the others this one too will be a form of what I dream, a structure of words, and not the flesh and bone tiger that beyond all myths paces the earth. I know these things quite well, yet nonetheless some force keeps driving me in this vague, unreasonable, and ancient quest, and I go on pursuing through the hours another tiger, the beast not found in verse.

—J. L. Borges, *The Other Tiger*, 1960

I have no time to describe my plans. I should say a good deal about The Hours, & my discovery; how I dig out beautiful caves behind my characters; I think that gives exactly what I want; humanity, humour, depth. The idea is that the caves shall connect, & each comes to daylight at the present moment.

—Virginia Woolf, in her diary, August 30, 1923

[illegible] like to [illegible]

[illegible]

and [illegible] know [illegible] well [illegible]

[illegible] hours [illegible]

[illegible]

— [illegible]

[illegible] the [illegible]

[illegible] that [illegible]

[illegible] the [illegible]

[illegible]

The Hours

Prologue

She hurries from the house, wearing a coat too heavy for the weather. It is 1941. Another war has begun. She has left a note for Leonard, and another for Vanessa. She walks purposefully toward the river, certain of what she'll do, but even now she is almost distracted by the sight of the downs, the church, and a scattering of sheep, incandescent, tinged with a faint hint of sulfur, grazing under a darkening sky. She pauses, watching the sheep and the sky, then walks on. The voices murmur behind her; bombers drone in the sky, though she looks for the planes and can't see them. She walks past one of the farm workers (is his name John?), a robust, small-headed man wearing a potato-colored vest, cleaning the ditch that runs through the osier bed. He looks up at her, nods, looks down again into the brown water. As she passes him on her way to the river she thinks of how successful he is, how fortunate, to be cleaning a ditch in an osier bed. She herself has failed. She is not a writer at all, really; she is merely a gifted eccentric. Patches of sky shine in puddles left over from last night's rain. Her shoes sink slightly into the soft earth. She has failed, and now the voices are back, muttering indistinctly just beyond the range of her vision, behind her, here, no, turn and they've gone somewhere else. The voices are back and the headache is approaching as surely as rain, the headache that will crush whatever is she and replace her with itself. The headache is approaching and it seems (is she or is she not conjuring them herself?) that the bombers have appeared again in the sky. She reaches the embankment, climbs over and down again to the river. There's a fisherman upriver, far away, he won't notice her, will he? She begins searching for a stone. She works quickly but methodically, as if she were following a recipe that must be obeyed scrupulously if it's to succeed at all. She selects one roughly the size and shape of a pig's skull. Even as she lifts it and forces it into one of the pockets of her coat (the fur collar tickles her neck), she can't help noticing the stone's cold chalkiness and its color, a milky brown with spots of green. She stands close to the edge of the river, which laps against the bank, filling the small irregularities in the mud with clear water that might be a different substance altogether from the yellow-brown, dappled stuff, solid-looking as a road, that extends so steadily from bank to bank. She steps forward. She does not remove her shoes. The water is cold, but not unbearably so. She pauses, standing in cold water up to her knees. She thinks of Leonard. She thinks of his hands and his face, the deep lines around his mouth.

She thinks of Vanessa, of the children, of Vita and Ethel: So many. They have all failed, haven't they? She is suddenly, immensely sorry for them. She imagines turning around, taking the stone out of her pocket, going back to the house. She could probably return in time to destroy the notes. She could live on; she could perform that final kindness. Standing knee-deep in the moving water, she decides against it. The voices are here, the headache is coming, and if she restores herself to the care of Leonard and Vanessa they won't let her go again, will they? She decides to insist that they let her go. She wades awkwardly (the bottom is mucky) out until she is up to her waist. She glances upriver at the fisherman, who is wearing a red jacket and who does not see her. The yellow surface of the river (more yellow than brown when seen this close) murkily reflects the sky. Here, then, is the last moment of true perception, a man fishing in a red jacket and a cloudy sky reflected on opaque water. Almost involuntarily (it feels involuntary, to her) she steps or stumbles forward, and the stone pulls her in. For a moment, still, it seems like nothing; it seems like another failure; just chill water she can easily swim back out of; but then the current wraps itself around her and takes her with such sudden, muscular force it feels as if a strong man has risen from the bottom, grabbed her legs and held them to his chest. It feels personal.

More than an hour later, her husband returns from the garden. "Madame went out," the maid says, plumping a shabby pillow that releases a miniature storm of down. "She said she'd be back soon."

Leonard goes upstairs to the sitting room to listen to the news. He finds a blue envelope, addressed to him, on the table. Inside is a letter.

Dearest,
I feel certain that I am going
mad again: I feel we can't go
through another of these terrible times.
And I shant recover this time. I begin
to hear voices, and cant concentrate.
So I am doing what seems the best thing to do. You have
given me
the greatest possible happiness. You
have been in every way all that anyone
could be. I dont think two
people could have been happier till
this terrible disease came. I cant
fight it any longer, I know that I am
spoiling your life, that without me you
could work. And you will I know.
You see I cant even write this properly. I
cant read. What I want to say is that
I owe all the happiness of my life to you.
You have been entirely patient with me &
incredibly good. I want to say that—
everybody knows it. If anybody could
have saved me it would have been you.
Everything has gone from me but the
certainty of your goodness. I

cant go on spoiling your life any longer. I dont think two people
could have been happier than we have been.
V.

Leonard races from the room, runs downstairs. He says to the maid, "I think something has happened to Mrs. Woolf. I think she may have tried to kill herself. Which way did she go? Did you see her leave the house?"

The maid, panicked, begins to cry. Leonard rushes out and goes to the river, past the church and the sheep, past the osier bed. At the riverbank he finds no one but a man in a red jacket, fishing.

She is borne quickly along by the current. She appears to be flying, a fantastic figure, arms outstretched, hair streaming, the tail of the fur coat billowing behind. She floats, heavily, through shafts of brown, granular light. She does not travel far. Her feet (the shoes are gone) strike the bottom occasionally, and when they do they summon up a sluggish cloud of muck, filled with the black silhouettes of leaf skeletons, that stands all but stationary in the water after she has passed along out of sight. Stripes of green-black weed catch in her hair and the fur of her coat, and for a while her eyes are blindfolded by a thick swatch of weed, which finally loosens itself and floats, twisting and untwisting and twisting again.

She comes to rest, eventually, against one of the pilings of the bridge at Southease. The current presses her, worries her, but she is firmly positioned at the base of the squat, square column, with her back to the river and her face against the stone. She curls there with one arm folded against her chest and the other afloat over the rise of her hip. Some distance above her is the bright, rippled surface. The sky reflects unsteadily there, white and heavy with clouds, traversed by the black cutout shapes of rooks. Cars and trucks rumble over the bridge. A small boy, no older than three, crossing the bridge with his mother, stops at the rail, crouches, and pushes the stick he's been carrying between the slats of the railing so it will fall into the water. His mother urges him along but he insists on staying awhile, watching the stick as the current takes it.

Here they are, on a day early in the Second World War: the boy and his mother on the bridge, the stick floating over the water's surface, and Virginia's body at the river's bottom, as if she is dreaming of the surface, the stick, the boy and his mother, the sky and the rooks. An olive-drab truck rolls across the bridge, loaded with soldiers in uniform, who wave to the boy who has just thrown the stick. He waves back. He demands that his mother pick him up so he can see the soldiers better; so he will be more visible to them. All this enters the bridge, resounds through its wood and stone, and enters Virginia's body. Her face, pressed sideways to the piling, absorbs it all: the truck and the soldiers, the mother and the child.

Mrs. Dalloway

There are still the flowers to buy. Clarissa feigns exasperation (though she loves doing errands like this), leaves Sally cleaning the bathroom, and runs out, promising to be back in half an hour.

It is New York City. It is the end of the twentieth century.

The vestibule door opens onto a June morning so fine and scrubbed Clarissa pauses at the threshold as she would at the edge of a pool, watching the turquoise water lapping at the tiles, the liquid nets of sun wavering in the blue depths. As if standing at the edge of a pool she delays for a moment the plunge, the quick membrane of chill, the plain shock of immersion. New York in its racket and stern brown decrepitude, its bottomless decline, always produces a few summer mornings like this; mornings invaded everywhere by an assertion of new life so determined it is almost comic, like a cartoon character that endures endless, hideous punishments and always emerges unburnt, unscarred, ready for more. This June, again, the trees along West Tenth Street have produced perfect little leaves from the squares of dog dirt and discarded wrappers in which they stand. Again the window box of the old woman next door, filled as it always is with faded red plastic geraniums pushed into the dirt, has sprouted a rogue dandelion.

What a thrill, what a shock, to be alive on a morning in June, prosperous, almost scandalously privileged, with a simple errand to run. She, Clarissa Vaughan, an ordinary person (at this age, why bother trying to deny it?), has flowers to buy and a party to give. As Clarissa steps down from the vestibule her shoe makes gritty contact with the red-brown, mica-studded stone of the first stair. She is fifty-two, just fifty-two, and in almost unnaturally good health. She feels every bit as good as she did that day in Wellfleet, at the age of eighteen, stepping out through the glass doors into a day very much like this one, fresh and almost painfully clear, rampant with growth. There were dragonflies zigzagging among the cattails. There was a grassy smell sharpened by pine sap. Richard came out behind her, put a hand on her shoulder, and said, "Why, hello, Mrs. Dalloway." The name Mrs. Dalloway had been Richard's idea—a conceit tossed off one drunken dormitory night as he assured her that Vaughan was not the proper name for her. She should, he'd said, be named after a great figure in literature, and while she'd argued for Isabel Archer or Anna Karenina, Richard had insisted that Mrs. Dalloway was the singular and obvious choice. There was the matter of her existing first name, a sign too obvious to ignore, and, more important, the larger question of fate. She, Clarissa, was clearly not destined to make a disastrous marriage or fall under the wheels of a train. She was destined to charm, to prosper. So Mrs. Dalloway it was and would be. "Isn't it beautiful?" Mrs. Dalloway said that morning to Richard. He answered, "Beauty is a whore, I like money better." He preferred wit. Clarissa, being the youngest, the only woman, felt she could afford a certain sentimentality. If it was late June, she and Richard would have been lovers. It would have been almost a full month since Richard left Louis's bed (Louis the farm-boy fantasy, the living embodiment of lazy-eyed carnality) and came into hers.

"Well, I happen to like beauty," she'd said. She'd lifted his hand from her shoulder, bit down on the tip of his index finger, a little harder than she'd meant to. She was eighteen, renamed. She could do what she liked.

Clarissa's shoes make their soft sandpaper sounds as she descends the stairs on her way to buy flowers. Why doesn't she feel more somber about Richard's perversely simultaneous good fortune ("an anguished, prophetic voice in American letters") and his decline ("You have no T-cells at all, none that we can detect")? What is wrong with her? She loves Richard, she thinks of him constantly, but she perhaps loves the day slightly more. She loves West Tenth Street on an ordinary summer morning. She feels like a sluttish widow, freshly peroxided under her black veil, with her eye on the eligible men at her husband's wake. Of the three of them—Louis, Richard, and Clarissa—Clarissa has always been the most hard-hearted, and the one most prone to romance. She's endured teasing on the subject for more than thirty years; she decided long ago to give in and enjoy her own voluptuous, undisciplined responses, which, as Richard put it, tend to be as unkind and adoring as those of a particularly irritating, precocious child. She knows that a poet like Richard would move sternly through the same morning, editing it, dismissing incidental ugliness along with incidental beauty, seeking the economic and historical truth behind these old brick town houses, the austere stone complications of the Episcopal church and the thin middle-aged man walking his Jack Russell terrier (they are suddenly ubiquitous along Fifth Avenue, these feisty, bowlegged little dogs), while she, Clarissa, simply enjoys without reason the houses, the church, the man, and the dog. It's childish, she knows. It lacks edge. If she were to express it publicly (now, at her age), this love of hers would consign her to the realm of the duped and the simpleminded, Christians with acoustic guitars or wives who've agreed to be harmless in exchange for their keep. Still, this indiscriminate love feels entirely serious to her, as if everything in the world is part of a vast, inscrutable intention and everything in the world has its own secret name, a name that cannot be conveyed in language but is simply the sight and feel of the thing itself. This determined, abiding fascination is what she thinks of as her soul (an embarrassing, sentimental word, but what else to call it?); the part that might conceivably survive the death of the body. Clarissa never speaks to anyone about any of that. She doesn't gush or chirp. She exclaims only over the obvious manifestations of beauty, and even then manages a certain aspect of adult restraint. Beauty is a whore, she sometimes says. I like money better.

Tonight she will give her party. She will fill the rooms of her apartment with food and flowers, with people of wit and influence. She will shepherd Richard through it, see that he doesn't overtire, and then she will escort him uptown to receive his prize.

She straightens her shoulders as she stands at the corner of Eighth Street and Fifth Avenue, waiting for the light. There she is, thinks Willie Bass, who passes her some mornings just about here. The old beauty, the old hippie, hair still long and defiantly gray, out on her morning rounds in jeans and a man's cotton shirt, some sort of ethnic slippers (India? Central America?) on her feet. She still has a certain sexiness; a certain bohemian, good-witch sort of charm; and yet this morning she makes a tragic sight, standing so straight in her big shirt and exotic shoes, resisting the pull of gravity, a female mammoth already up to its knees in the tar, taking a rest between efforts, standing bulky and proud, almost nonchalant, pretending to contemplate the tender grasses waiting on the far bank when it is beginning to know for certain that it will remain here, trapped and alone, after dark, when the jackals come out. She waits patiently for the light. She must have been spectacular twenty-five years ago; men must have died happy in her arms. Willie Bass is proud of his ability to discern the history of a face; to understand that those who are now old were once young. The light changes and he walks on.

Clarissa crosses Eighth Street. She loves, helplessly, the dead television set abandoned on the curb alongside a single white patent-leather pump. She loves the vendor's cart piled with broccoli and peaches and mangoes, each labeled with an index card that offers a price amid abundances of punctuation: "$1.49!!" "3 for ONE Dollar!?!" "50 Cents EA.!!!!!" Ahead, under the Arch, an old woman in a dark, neatly tailored dress appears to be singing, stationed precisely between the twin statues of George Washington, as warrior and politician, both faces destroyed by weather. It's the city's crush and heave that move you; its intricacy; its endless life. You know the story about Manhattan as a wilderness purchased for strings of beads but you find it impossible not to believe that it has always been a city; that if you dug beneath it you would find the ruins of another, older city, and then another and another. Under the cement and grass of the park (she has crossed into the park now, where the old woman throws back her head and sings) lay the bones of those buried in the potter's field that was simply paved over, a hundred years ago, to make Washington Square. Clarissa walks over the bodies of the dead as men whisper offers of drugs (not to her) and three black girls whiz past on roller skates and the old woman sings, tunelessly, *iiiiiii*. Clarissa is skittish and jubilant about her luck, her good shoes (on sale at Barney's, but still); here after all is the sturdy squalor of the park, visible even under its coat of grass and flowers; here are the drug dealers (would they kill you if it came to that?) and the lunatics, the stunned and baffled, the people whose luck, if they ever had any, has run out. Still, she loves the world for being rude and indestructible, and she knows other people must love it too, poor as well as rich, though no one speaks specifically of the reasons. Why else do we struggle to go on living, no matter how compromised, no matter how harmed? Even if we're further gone than Richard; even if we're fleshless, blazing with lesions, shitting in the sheets; still, we want desperately to live. It has to do with all this, she thinks. Wheels buzzing on concrete, the roil and shock of it; sheets of bright spray blowing from the fountain as young shirtless men toss a Frisbee and vendors (from Peru, from Guatemala) send pungent, meaty smoke up from their quilted silver carts; old men and women straining after the sun from their benches, speaking softly to each other, shaking their heads; the bleat of car horns and the strum of guitars (that ragged group over there, three boys and a girl, could they possibly be playing "Eight Miles High"?); leaves shimmering on the trees; a spotted dog chasing pigeons and a passing radio playing "Always love you" as the woman in the dark dress stands under the arch singing *iiiii*.

She crosses the plaza, receives a quick spatter from the fountain, and here comes Walter Hardy, muscular in shorts and a white tank top, performing his jaunty, athletic stride for Washington Square Park. "Hey, Clare," Walter calls jockishly, and they pass through an awkward moment about how to kiss. Walter aims his lips for Clarissa's and she instinctively turns her own mouth away, offering her cheek instead. Then she catches herself and turns back a half second too late, so that Walter's lips touch only the corner of her mouth. I'm so prim, Clarissa thinks; so grandmotherly. I swoon over the beauties of the world but am reluctant, simply as a matter of reflex, to kiss a friend on the mouth. Richard told her, thirty years ago, that under her pirate-girl veneer lay all the makings of a good suburban wife, and she is now revealed to herself as a meager spirit, too conventional, the cause of much suffering. No wonder her daughter resents her.

"Nice to see you," Walter says. Clarissa knows—she can practically see—that Walter is, at this moment, working mentally through a series of intricate calibrations regarding her personal significance. Yes, she's the woman in the book, the subject of a much-anticipated novel by an almost legendary writer, but the book failed, didn't it? It was curtly reviewed; it slipped silently beneath the waves. She is, Walter decides, like a deposed aristocrat, interesting without being particularly important. She sees him arrive at his decision. She smiles.

"What are you doing in New York on a Saturday?" she asks.

"Evan and I are staying in town this weekend," he says. "He's feeling so much better on this new cocktail, he says he wants to go dancing tonight."

"Isn't that a little much?"

"I'll keep an eye on him. I won't let him overdo it. He just wants to be out in the world again."

"Do you think he'd feel up to coming to our place this evening? We're having a little party for Richard, in honor of the Carrouthers Prize."

"Oh. Great."

"You do know about it, don't you?"

"Sure."

"It's not some annual thing. They have no quota to fill, like the Nobel and all those others. They simply award it when they become aware of someone whose career seems undeniably significant."

"That's great."

"Yes," she says. She adds, after a moment, "The last recipient was Ashbery. The last before him were Merrill, Rich, and Merwin."

A shadow passes over Walter's broad, innocent face. Clarissa wonders: Is he puzzling over the names? Or could he, could he possibly, be envious? Does he imagine that he himself might be a contender for an honor like that?

"I'm sorry I didn't tell you about the party sooner," she says. "It just never occurred to me you'd be around. You and Evan are never in town on the weekends."

Walter says of course he'll come, and he'll bring Evan if Evan feels up to it, though Evan, of course, may choose to husband his energies for dancing. Richard will be furious to hear that Walter has been invited, and Sally will certainly side with him. Clarissa understands. Little in the world is less mysterious than the disdain people often feel for Walter Hardy, who's elected to turn forty-six in baseball caps and Nikes; who makes an obscene amount of money writing romance novels about love and loss among perfectly muscled young men; who can stay out all night dancing to house music, blissful and inexhaustible as a German shepherd retrieving a stick. You see men like Walter all over Chelsea and the Village, men who insist, at thirty or forty or older, that they have always been chipper and confident, powerful of body; that they've never been strange children, never taunted or despised. Richard argues that eternally youthful gay men do more harm to the cause than do men who seduce little boys, and yes, it's true that Walter brings no shadow of adult irony or cynicism, nothing remotely profound, to his interest in fame and fashions, the latest restaurant. Yet it is just this greedy innocence Clarissa appreciates. Don't we love children, in part, because they live outside the realm of cynicism and irony? Is it so terrible for a man to want more youth, more pleasure? Besides, Walter is not corrupt; not exactly corrupt. He writes the best books he can—books full of romance and sacrifice, courage in the face of adversity—and surely they must offer real comfort to any number of people. His name appears constantly on invitations to fund-raisers and on letters of protest; he writes embarrassingly lavish blurbs for younger writers. He takes good, faithful care of Evan. These days, Clarissa believes, you measure people first by their kindness and their capacity for devotion. You get tired, sometimes, of wit and intellect; everybody's little display of genius. She refuses to stop enjoying Walter Hardy's shameless shallowness, even if it drives Sally to distraction and has actually inspired Richard to wonder out loud if she, Clarissa, isn't more than a little vain and foolish herself.

"Good," Clarissa says. "You know where we live, right? Five o'clock."

"Five o'clock."

"It needs to be early. The ceremony's at eight, we're having the party before instead of after. Richard can't manage late nights."

"Right. Five o'clock. See you then." Walter squeezes Clarissa's hand and walks on with a swaggering two-step, a demonstration of hefty vitality. It's a cruel joke, of a sort, inviting Walter to Richard's party, but Walter, after all, is alive, just as Clarissa is, on a morning in June, and he'll feel horribly snubbed if he finds out (and he seems to find everything out) Clarissa spoke to him the day of the party and deliberately failed to mention it. Wind worries the leaves, showing the brighter, grayer green of their undersides, and Clarissa wishes, suddenly and with surprising urgency, that Richard were here beside her, right now—not Richard as he's become but the Richard of ten years ago; Richard the fearless, ceaseless talker; Richard the gadfly. She wants the argument she and that Richard would have had about Walter. Before Richard's decline, Clarissa always fought with him. Richard actually worried over questions of good and evil, and he never, not in twenty years, fully abandoned the notion that Clarissa's decision to live with Sally represents, if not some workaday manifestation of deep corruption, at least a weakness on her part that indicts (though Richard would never admit this) women in general, since he seems to have decided early on that Clarissa stands not only for herself but for the gifts and frailties of her entire sex. Richard has always been Clarissa's most rigorous, infuriating companion, her best friend, and if Richard were still himself, untouched by illness, they could be together right now, arguing about Walter Hardy and the quest for eternal youth, about how gay men have taken to imitating the boys who tortured them in high school. The old Richard would be capable of talking for half an hour or more about the various possible interpretations of the inept copy of Botticelli's Venus being drawn by a young black man with chalk on the concrete, and if that Richard had noticed the windblown plastic bag that billowed against the white sky, rippling like a jellyfish, he'd have carried on about chemicals and endless profits, the hand that takes. He'd have wanted to talk about how the bag (say it had contained potato chips and overripe bananas; say it had been thoughtlessly discarded by a harassed, indigent mother as she left a store amid her gaggle of quarreling children) will blow into the Hudson and float all the way to the ocean, where eventually a sea turtle, a creature that could live a hundred years, will mistake it for a jellyfish, eat the bag, and die. It wouldn't have been impossible for Richard to segue, somehow, from that subject directly to Sally; to inquire after her health and happiness with pointed formality. He had a habit of asking about Sally after one of his tirades, as if Sally were some sort of utterly banal safe haven; as if Sally herself (Sally the stoic, the tortured, the subtly wise) were harmless and insipid in the way of a house on a quiet street or a good, solid, reliable car. Richard will neither admit to nor recover from his dislike of her, never; he will never discard his private conviction that Clarissa has, at heart, become a society wife, and never mind the fact that she and Sally do not attempt to disguise their love for anyone's sake, or that Sally is a devoted, intelligent woman, a producer of public television, for heaven's sake—how much more hardworking and socially responsible, how much more dramatically underpaid, does she need to be? Never mind the good, flagrantly unprofitable books Clarissa insists on publishing alongside the pulpier items that pay her way. Never mind her politics, all her work with PWAs.

Clarissa crosses Houston Street and thinks she might pick up a little something for Evan, to acknowledge his tentatively returning health. Not flowers; if flowers are subtly wrong for the deceased they're disastrous for the ill. But what? The shops of SoHo are full of party dresses and jewelry and Biedermeier; nothing to take to an imperious, clever young man who might or might not, with the help of a battery of drugs, live out his normal span. What does anyone want? Clarissa passes a shop and thinks of buying a dress for Julia, she'd look stunning in that little black one with the Anna Magnani straps, but Julia doesn't wear dresses, she insists on spending her youth, the brief period in which one can wear anything at all, stomping around in men's undershirts and leather lace-ups the size of cinder blocks. (Why does her daughter tell her so little? What happened to the ring Clarissa gave her for her eighteenth birthday?) Here's that good little bookstore on Spring Street. Maybe Evan would like a book. Displayed in the window is one (only one!) of Clarissa's, the English one (criminal, how she'd had to battle for a printing of ten thousand copies and, worse, how it looks as if they'll be lucky to sell five), alongside the South American family saga she lost to a bigger house, which will clearly fail to earn out because, for mysterious reasons, it is respected but not loved. There is the new biography of Robert Mapplethorpe, the poems of Louise Glück, but nothing seems right. They are all, at once, too general and too specific. You want to give him the book of his own life, the book that will locate him, parent him, arm him for the changes. You can't show up with celebrity gossip, can you? You can't bring the story of an embittered English novelist or the fates of seven sisters in Chile, however beautifully written, and Evan is about as likely to read poetry as he is to take up painting on china plates.

There is no comfort, it seems, in the world of objects, and Clarissa fears that art, even the greatest of it (even Richard's three volumes of poetry and his single, unreadable novel), belong stubbornly to the world of objects. Standing in front of the bookstore window, she is visited by an old memory, a tree branch tapping against a window as, from somewhere else (downstairs?), faint music, the low moan of a jazz band, started up on a phonograph. It is not her first memory (that seems to involve a snail crawling over the lip of a curb) or even her second (her mother's straw sandals, or maybe the two are reversed), but this memory more than any other feels urgent and deeply, almost supernaturally comforting. Clarissa would have been in a house in Wisconsin, probably; one of the many her parents rented during the summers (rarely the same one twice—each proved to have some defect for her mother to stitch into her ongoing narrative, the Vaughan Family's Trail of Tears Tour of the Wisconsin Dells). Clarissa would have been three or four, in a house to which she would never return, about which she retains no recollection except this, utterly distinct, clearer than some things that happened yesterday: a branch tapping at a window as the sound of horns began; as if the tree, being unsettled by wind, had somehow caused the music. It seems that at that moment she began to inhabit the world; to understand the promises implied by an order larger than human happiness, though it contained human happiness along with every other emotion. The branch and the music matter more to her than do all the books in the store window. She wants for Evan and she wants for herself a book that can carry what that singular memory carries. She stands looking at the books and at her reflection superimposed on the glass (she still looks all right, handsome now instead of pretty—when will the crepe and gauntness, the shriveled lips, of her old woman's face begin to emerge?), and then she walks on, regretting the lovely little black dress she can't buy for her daughter because Julia is in thrall to a queer theorist and insists on T-shirts and combat boots. You respect Mary Krull, she really gives you no choice, living as she does on the verge of poverty, going to jail for her various causes, lecturing passionately at NYU about the sorry masquerade known as gender. You want to like her, you struggle to, but she is finally too despotic in her intellectual and moral intensity, her endless demonstration of cutting-edge, leather-jacketed righteousness. You know she mocks you, privately, for your comforts and your quaint (she must consider them quaint) notions about lesbian identity. You grow weary of being treated as the enemy simply because you are not young anymore; because you dress unexceptionally. You want to scream at Mary Krull that it doesn't make that much difference; you want her to come inside your head for a few days and feel the worries and sorrows, the nameless fear. You believe—you *know*—that you and Mary Krull suffer from the same mortal sickness, the same queasiness of soul, and with one more turn of the dial you might have been friends, but as it is she's come to claim your daughter and you sit in your comfortable apartment hating her as much as any Republican father would. Clarissa's father, gentle almost to the point of translucence, loved seeing women in little black dresses. Her father grew exhausted; he gave up his cogency the way he often gave up arguments, simply because it was easier to agree. Up ahead, on MacDougal, a company is shooting a movie amid the usual welter of trailers and equipment trucks, the banks of white lights. Here is the ordinary world, a movie being shot, a Puerto Rican boy cranking open the awning of a restaurant with a silver pole. Here is the world, and you live in it, and are grateful. You try to be grateful.

She pushes open the florist's door, which always sticks slightly, and walks in, a tall woman, broad-shouldered amid the bunches of roses and hyacinths, the mossy flats of paperwhites, the orchids trembling on their stalks. Barbara, who has worked in the shop for years, says hello. After a pause, she offers her cheek for a kiss.

"Hello," Clarissa says. Her lips touch Barbara's skin and the moment is suddenly, unexpectedly perfect. She stands in the dim, deliciously cool little shop that is like a temple, solemn in its abundance, its bunches of dried flowers hanging from the ceiling and its rack of ribbons trailing against the back wall. There was that branch tapping the windowpane and there was another, though she'd been older, five or six, in her own bedroom, this branch covered with red leaves, and she can remember thinking back reverently, even then, to that earlier branch, the one that had seemed to excite the music downstairs; she remembers loving the autumn branch for reminding her of the earlier branch, tapping against the window of a house to which she would never return, which she could not otherwise remember in any of its particulars. Now she is here, in the flower shop, where poppies drift white and apricot on long, hairy stems. Her mother, who kept a tin of snowy French mints in her purse, pursed her lips and called Clarissa crazy, a crazy girl, in a tone of flirtatious admiration.

"How are you?" Barbara asks.

"Fine, just fine," she says. "We're having a little party tonight, for a friend who's just won this big-deal literary award."

"The Pulitzer?"

"No. It's called the Carrouthers Prize."

Barbara offers a blank expression that Clarissa understands is meant as a smile. Barbara is forty or so, a pale, ample woman who came to New York to sing opera. Something about her face—the square jaw or the stern, inexpressive eyes—reminds you that people looked essentially the same a hundred years ago.

"We're a little low right now," she says. "There've been about fifty weddings this week."

"I don't need much," Clarissa says. "Just a few bunches of something or other." Clarissa feels inexplicably guilty about not being a better friend to Barbara, though they know each other only as customer and saleswoman. Clarissa buys all her flowers from Barbara, and sent her a card a year ago, when she heard of her breast-cancer scare. Barbara's career has not gone as planned; she lives somehow on her hourly wages (a tenement, probably, with the bathtub in the kitchen) and she has escaped cancer, this time. For a moment Mary Krull hovers over the lilies and roses, preparing to be appalled at what Clarissa will spend.

"We've got some beautiful hydrangeas," Barbara says.

"Let's see." Clarissa goes to the cooler and chooses flowers, which Barbara pulls from their containers and holds, dripping, in her arms. In the nineteenth century she'd have been a country wife, gentle and unremarkable, dissatisfied, standing in a garden. Clarissa chooses peonies and stargazer lilies, cream-colored roses, does not want the hydrangeas (guilt, guilt, it looks like you never outgrow it), and is considering irises (are irises somehow a little . . . outdated?) when a huge shattering sound comes from the street outside.

"What was that?" Barbara says. She and Clarissa go to the window.

"I think it's the movie people."

"Probably. They've been filming out there all morning."

"Do you know what it is?"

"No," she says, and she turns away from the window with a certain elderly rectitude, holding her armful of flowers just as the ghost of her earlier self, a hundred years ago, would have turned from the rattle and creak of a carriage passing by, full of perfectly dressed picnickers from a distant city. Clarissa remains, looking out at the welter of trucks and trailers. Suddenly the door to one of the trailers opens, and a famous head emerges. It is a woman's head, quite a distance away, seen in profile, like the head on a coin, and while Clarissa cannot immediately identify her (Meryl Streep? Vanessa Redgrave?) she knows without question that the woman is a movie star. She knows by her aura of regal assurance, and by the eagerness with which one of the prop men speaks to her (inaudibly to Clarissa) about the source of the noise. The woman's head quickly withdraws, the door to the trailer closes again, but she leaves behind her an unmistakable sense of watchful remonstrance, as if an angel had briefly touched the surface of the world with one sandaled foot, asked if there was any trouble and, being told all was well, had resumed her place in the ether with skeptical gravity, having reminded the children of earth that they are just barely trusted to manage their own business, and that further carelessness will not go unremarked.

prairie. [illegible]

[illegible]

about the [illegible]

[illegible] the surface of the world with [illegible]

very well [illegible]

[illegible]

Mrs. Woolf

Mrs. Dalloway said something (what?), and got the flowers herself.

It is a suburb of London. It is 1923.

Virginia awakens. This might be another way to begin, certainly; with Clarissa going on an errand on a day in June, instead of soldiers marching off to lay the wreath in Whitehall. But is it the right beginning? Is it a little too ordinary? Virginia lies quietly in her bed, and sleep takes her again so quickly she is not conscious of falling back to sleep at all. It seems, suddenly, that she is not in her bed but in a park; a park impossibly verdant, green beyond green—a Platonic vision of a park, at once homely and the seat of mystery, implying as parks do that while the old woman in the shawl dozes on the slatted bench something alive and ancient, something neither kind nor unkind, exulting only in continuance, knits together the green world of farms and meadows, forests and parks. Virginia moves through the park without quite walking; she floats through it, a feather of perception, unbodied. The park reveals to her its banks of lilies and peonies, its graveled paths bordered by cream-colored roses. A stone maiden, smoothed by weather, stands at the edge of a clear pool and muses into the water. Virginia moves through the park as if impelled by a cushion of air; she is beginning to understand that another park lies beneath this one, a park of the underworld, more marvelous and terrible than this; it is the root from which these lawns and arbors grow. It is the true idea of the park, and it is nothing so simple as beautiful. She can see people now: a Chinese man stooping to pick something up off the grass, a little girl waiting. Up ahead, on a circle of newly turned earth, a woman sings.

Virginia awakens again. She is here, in her bedroom at Hogarth House. Gray light fills the room; muted, steel-toned; it lies with a gray-white, liquid life on her coverlet. It silvers the green walls. She has dreamed of a park and she has dreamed of a line for her new book—what was it? Flowers; something to do with flowers. Or something to do with a park? Was someone singing? No, the line is gone, and it doesn't matter, really, because she still has the feeling it left behind. She knows she can get up and write.

She rises from her bed and goes into the bathroom. Leonard is already up; he may already be at work. In the bathroom, she washes her face. She does not look directly into the oval mirror that hangs above the basin. She is aware of her reflected movements in the glass but does not permit herself to look. The mirror is dangerous; it sometimes shows her the dark manifestation of air that matches her body, takes her form, but stands behind, watching her, with porcine eyes and wet, hushed breathing. She washes her face and does not look, certainly not this morning, not when the work is waiting for her and she is anxious to join it the way she might join a party that had already started downstairs, a party full of wit and beauty certainly but full, too, of something finer than wit or beauty; something mysterious and golden; a spark of profound celebration, of life itself, as silks rustle across polished floors and secrets are whispered under the music. She, Virginia, could be a girl in a new dress, about to go down to a party, about to appear on the stairs, fresh and full of hope. No, she will not look in the mirror. She finishes washing her face.

When she is finished in the bathroom she descends into the dusky morning quiet of the hall. She wears her pale blue housecoat. Night still resides here. Hogarth House is always nocturnal, even with its chaos of papers and books, its bright hassocks and Persian rugs. It is not dark in itself but it seems to be illuminated against darkness, even as the wan, early sun shines between the curtains and cars and carriages rumble by on Paradise Road.

Virginia pours herself a cup of coffee in the dining room, walks quietly downstairs, but does not go to Nelly in the kitchen. This morning, she wants to get straight to work without risking exposure to Nelly's bargainings and grievances. It could be a good day; it needs to be treated carefully. Balancing the cup on its saucer, she goes into the printing room. Leonard is sitting at his desk, reading page proofs. It is too early yet for Ralph or Marjorie.

Leonard looks up at her, still wearing, for a moment, the scowl he has brought to the proofs. It is an expression she trusts and fears, his eyes blazing and impenetrably dark under his heavy brows, the corners of his mouth turned down in an expression of judgment that is severe but not in any way petulant or trivial—the frown of a deity, all-seeing and weary, hoping for the best from humankind, knowing just how much to expect. It is the expression he brings to all written work, including, and especially, her own. As he looks at her, though, the expression fades almost immediately and is replaced by the milder, kinder face of the husband who has nursed her through her worst periods, who does not demand what she can't provide and who urges on her, sometimes successfully, a glass of milk every morning at eleven.

"Good morning," she says.

"Good morning. How was your sleep?"

How *was* your sleep, he asks, as if sleep were not an act but a creature that could be either docile or fierce. Virginia says, "It was uneventful. Are those Tom's?"

"Yes."

"How do they look?"

He scowls again. "I've found an error already, and I'm not quite through the second page."

"One error at the beginning is quite likely just that. It's early in the day to be so bent on irritation, don't you think?"

"Have you had breakfast?" he asks.

"Yes."

"Liar."

"I'm having coffee with cream for breakfast. It's enough."

"It's far from enough. I'm going to have Nelly bring you a bun and some fruit."

"If you send Nelly in to interrupt me I won't be responsible for my actions."

"You must eat," he says. "It doesn't have to be much."

"I'll eat later. I'm going to work now."

He hesitates, then nods grudgingly. He does not, will not, interfere with her work. Still, Virginia refusing to eat is not a good sign.

"You will have lunch," he says. "A true lunch, soup, pudding, and all. By force, if it comes to that."

"I will have lunch," she says, impatiently but without true anger. She stands tall, haggard, marvelous in her housecoat, the coffee steaming in her hand. He is still, at times, astonished by her. She may be the most intelligent woman in England, he thinks. Her books may be read for centuries. He believes this more ardently than does anyone else. And she is his wife. She is Virginia Stephen, pale and tall, startling as a Rembrandt or a Velázquez, appearing twenty years ago at her brother's rooms in Cambridge in a white dress, and she is Virginia Woolf, standing before him right now. She has aged dramatically, just this year, as if a layer of air has leaked out from under her skin. She's grown craggy and worn. She's begun to look as if she's carved from very porous, gray-white marble. She is still regal, still exquisitely formed, still possessed of her formidable lunar radiance, but she is suddenly no longer beautiful.

"All right," he says. "I'm going to soldier on here."

She goes back upstairs stealthily, so as not to attract Nelly (why does she always feel so secretive around servants, so guilty of crimes?). She gets to her study, quietly closes the door. Safe. She opens the curtains. Outside, beyond the glass, Richmond continues in its decent, peaceful dream of itself. Flowers and hedges are attended to; shutters are repainted before they require it. The neighbors, whom she does not know, do whatever it is they do behind the blinds and shutters of their red brick villa. She can only think of dim rooms and a listless, overcooked smell. She turns from the window. If she can remain strong and clear, if she can keep on weighing at least nine and a half stone, Leonard will be persuaded to move back to London. The rest cure, these years among the delphinium beds and the red suburban villas, will be pronounced a success, and she will be deemed fit for the city again. Lunch, yes; she will have lunch. She should have breakfast but she can't bear the interruption it would entail, the contact with Nelly's mood. She will write for an hour or so, then eat something. Not eating is a vice, a drug of sorts—with her stomach empty she feels quick and clean, clearheaded, ready for a fight. She sips her coffee, sets it down, stretches her arms. This is one of the most singular experiences, waking on what feels like a good day, preparing to work but not yet actually embarked. At this moment there are infinite possibilities, whole hours ahead. Her mind hums. This morning she may penetrate the obfuscation, the clogged pipes, to reach the gold. She can feel it inside her, an all but indescribable second self, or rather a parallel, purer self. If she were religious, she would call it the soul. It is more than the sum of her intellect and her emotions, more than the sum of her experiences, though it runs like veins of brilliant metal through all three. It is an inner faculty that recognizes the animating mysteries of the world because it is made of the same substance, and when she is very fortunate she is able to write directly through that faculty. Writing in that state is the most profound satisfaction she knows, but her access to it comes and goes without warning. She may pick up her pen and follow it with her hand as it moves across the paper; she may pick up her pen and find that she's merely herself, a woman in a housecoat holding a pen, afraid and uncertain, only mildly competent, with no idea about where to begin or what to write.

She picks up her pen.

Mrs. Dalloway said she would buy the flowers herself.

Mrs. Brown

Mrs. Dalloway said she would buy the flowers herself.

For Lucy had her work cut out for her. The doors would have to be taken off their hinges; Rumpelmayer's men were coming. And then, thought Clarissa Dalloway, what a morning—fresh as if issued to children on a beach.

It is Los Angeles. It is 1949.

Laura Brown is trying to lose herself. No, that's not it exactly—she is trying to keep herself by gaining entry into a parallel world. She lays the book face down on her chest. Already her bedroom (no, *their* bedroom) feels more densely inhabited, more actual, because a character named Mrs. Dalloway is on her way to buy flowers. Laura glances at the clock on the nightstand. It's well past seven. Why did she buy this clock, this hideous thing, with its square green face in a rectangular black Bakelite sarcophagus—how could she ever have thought it was smart? She should not be permitting herself to read, not this morning of all mornings; not on Dan's birthday. She should be out of bed, showered and dressed, fixing breakfast for Dan and Richie. She can hear them downstairs, her husband making his own breakfast, ministering to Richie. She should be there, shouldn't she? She should be standing before the stove in her new robe, full of simple, encouraging talk. Still, when she opened her eyes a few minutes ago (after seven already!)—when she still half inhabited her dream, some sort of pulsating machinery in the remote distance, a steady pounding like a gigantic mechanical heart, which seemed to be drawing nearer—she felt the dank sensation around her, the nowhere feeling, and knew it was going to be a difficult day. She knew she was going to have trouble believing in herself, in the rooms of her house, and when she glanced over at this new book on her nightstand, stacked atop the one she finished last night, she reached for it automatically, as if reading were the singular and obvious first task of the day, the only viable way to negotiate the transit from sleep to obligation. Because she is pregnant, she is allowed these lapses. She is allowed, for now, to read unreasonably, to linger in bed, to cry or grow furious over nothing.

She will make up for breakfast by baking Dan a perfect birthday cake; by ironing the good cloth; by setting a big bouquet of flowers (roses?) in the middle of the table, and surrounding it with gifts. That should compensate, shouldn't it?

She will read one more page. One more page, to calm and locate herself, then she'll get out of bed.

What a lark! What a plunge! For so it had always seemed to her, when, with a little squeak of the hinges, which she could hear now, she had burst open the French windows and plunged at Bourton into the open air. How fresh, how calm, stiller than this of course, the air was in the early morning; like the flap of a wave; the kiss of a wave; chill and sharp and yet (for a girl of eighteen as she then was) solemn, feeling as she did, standing there at the open window, that something awful was about to happen; looking at the flowers, at the trees with the smoke winding off them and the rooks rising, falling; standing and looking until Peter Walsh said, "Musing among the vegetables?"—was that it?—"I prefer men to cauliflowers"—was that it? He must have said it at breakfast one morning when she had gone out on to the terrace—Peter Walsh. He would be back from India one of these days, June or July, she forgot which, for his letters were awfully dull; it was his sayings one remembered; his eyes, his pocket-knife, his smile, his grumpiness and, when millions of things had utterly vanished—how strange it was!—a few sayings like this about cabbages.

She inhales deeply. It is so beautiful; it is so much more than . . . well, than almost anything, really. In another world, she might have spent her whole life reading. But this is the new world, the rescued world—there's not much room for idleness. So much has been risked and lost; so many have died. Less than five years ago Dan himself was believed to have died, at Anzio, and when he was revealed two days later to be alive after all (he and some poor boy from Arcadia had had the same name), it seemed he had been resurrected. He seemed to have returned, still sweet-tempered, still smelling like himself, from the realm of the dead (the stories you heard then about Italy, about Saipan and Okinawa, about Japanese mothers who killed their children and themselves rather than be taken prisoner), and when he came back to California he was received as something more than an ordinary hero. He could (in the words of his own alarmed mother) have had anyone, any pageant winner, any vivacious and compliant girl, but through some obscure and possibly perverse genius had kissed, courted, and proposed to his best friend's older sister, the bookworm, the foreign-looking one with the dark, close-set eyes and the Roman nose, who had never been sought after or cherished; who had always been left alone, to read. What could she say but yes? How could she deny a handsome, good-hearted boy, practically a member of the family, who had come back from the dead?

So now she is Laura Brown. Laura Zielski, the solitary girl, the incessant reader, is gone, and here in her place is Laura Brown.

One more page, she decides; just one more. She isn't ready yet; the tasks that lie ahead (putting on her robe, brushing her hair, going down to the kitchen) are still too thin, too elusive. She will permit herself another minute here, in bed, before entering the day. She will allow herself just a little more time. She is taken by a wave of feeling, a sea-swell, that rises from under her breast and buoys her, floats her gently, as if she were a sea creature thrown back from the sand where it had beached itself—as if she had been returned from a realm of crushing gravity to her true medium, the suck and swell of saltwater, that weightless brilliance.

She stiffened a little on the kerb, waiting for Durtnall's van to pass. A charming woman, Scrope Purvis thought her (knowing her as one does know people who live next door to one in Westminster); a touch of the bird about her, of the jay, blue-green, light, vivacious, though she was over fifty, and grown very white since her illness. There she perched, never seeing him, waiting to cross, very upright.

For having lived in Westminster—how many years now? over twenty,—one feels even in the midst of the traffic, or waking at night, Clarissa was positive, a particular hush, or solemnity; an indescribable pause; a suspense (but that might be her heart, affected, they said, by influenza) before Big Ben strikes. There! Out it boomed. First a warning, musical; then the hour, irrevocable. The leaden circles dissolved in the air. Such fools we are, she thought, crossing Victoria Street. For Heaven only knows why one loves it so, how one sees it so, making it up, building it round one, tumbling it, creating it every moment afresh; but the veriest frumps, the most dejected of miseries sitting on doorsteps (drink their downfall) do the same; can't be dealt with, she felt positive, by Acts of Parliament for that very reason: they love life. In people's eyes, in the swing, tramp, and trudge; in the bellow and the uproar, the carriages, motor cars, omnibuses, vans, sandwich men shuffling and swinging; brass bands; barrel organs; in the triumph and the jingle and the strange high singing of some aeroplane overhead was what she loved; life; London; this moment of June.

How, Laura wonders, could someone who was able to write a sentence like that—who was able to feel everything contained in a sentence like that—come to kill herself? What in the world is wrong with people? Summoning resolve, as if she were about to dive into cold water, Laura closes the book and lays it on the nightstand. She does not dislike her child, does not dislike her husband. She will rise and be cheerful.

At least, she thinks, she does not read mysteries or romances.

At least she continues to improve her mind. Right now she is reading Virginia Woolf, all of Virginia Woolf, book by book—she is fascinated by the idea of a woman like that, a woman of such brilliance, such strangeness, such immeasurable sorrow; a woman who had genius but still filled her pocket with a stone and waded out into a river. She, Laura, likes to imagine (it's one of her most closely held secrets) that she has a touch of brilliance herself, just a hint of it, though she knows most people probably walk around with similar hopeful suspicions curled up like tiny fists inside them, never divulged. She wonders, while she pushes a cart through the supermarket or has her hair done, if the other women aren't all thinking, to some degree or other, the same thing: Here is the brilliant spirit, the woman of sorrows, the woman of transcendent joys, who would rather be elsewhere, who has consented to perform simple and essentially foolish tasks, to examine tomatoes, to sit under a hair dryer, because it is her art and her duty. Because the war is over, the world has survived, and we are here, all of us, making homes, having and raising children, creating not just books or paintings but a whole world—a world of order and harmony where children are safe (if not happy), where men who have seen horrors beyond imagining, who have acted bravely and well, come home to lighted windows, to perfume, to plates and napkins.

What a lark! What a plunge!

Laura gets out of bed. It is a hot, white morning in June. She can hear her husband moving around downstairs. A metal lid kisses the rim of its pan. She takes her robe, pale aqua chenille, from the newly reupholstered chair and the chair appears, squat and fat, skirted, its nubbly salmon-colored fabric held down by cord and salmon-colored buttons in a diamond pattern. In the morning heat of June, with the robe whisked away, the chair in its bold new fabric seems surprised to find itself a chair at all.

She brushes her teeth, brushes her hair, and starts downstairs. She pauses several treads from the bottom, listening, waiting; she is again possessed (it seems to be getting worse) by a dream-like feeling, as if she is standing in the wings, about to go onstage and perform in a play for which she is not appropriately dressed, and for which she has not adequately rehearsed. What, she wonders, is wrong with her. This is her husband in the kitchen; this is her little boy. All the man and boy require of her is her presence and, of course, her love. She conquers the desire to go quietly back upstairs, to her bed and book. She conquers her irritation at the sound of her husband's voice, saying something to Richie about napkins (why does his voice remind her sometimes of a potato being grated?). She descends the last three stairs, crosses the narrow foyer, enters the kitchen.

She thinks of the cake she will bake, the flowers she'll buy. She thinks of roses surrounded by gifts.

Her husband has made the coffee, poured cereal for himself and their son. On the tabletop, a dozen white roses offer their complex, slightly sinister beauty. Through the clear glass vase Laura can see the bubbles, fine as grains of sand, clinging to their stems. Beside the roses stand cereal box and milk carton, with their words and pictures.

"Good morning," her husband says, raising his eyebrows as if he is surprised but delighted to see her.

"Happy birthday," she says.

"Thank you."

"Oh, Dan. Roses. On *your* birthday. You're too much, really."

She sees him see that she is angry. She smiles.

"It wouldn't mean much of anything without you, would it?" he says.

"But you should have woken me. Really."

He looks at Richie, lifts his brows another centimeter, so that his forehead is creased and his lustrous black hair twitches slightly. "We thought it'd be better if you slept in a little, didn't we?" he says.

Richie, three years old, says, "Yes." He nods avidly.

He wears blue pajamas. He is happy to see her, and more than happy; he is rescued, resurrected, transported by love. Laura reaches into the pocket of her robe for a cigarette, changes her mind, raises her hand instead to her hair. It is almost perfect, it is almost enough, to be a young mother in a yellow kitchen touching her thick, dark hair, pregnant with another child. There are leaf shadows on the curtains; there is fresh coffee.

"G'morning, Bug," she says to Richie.

"I'm having cereal," he says. He grins. It could be said that he leers. He is transparently smitten with her; he is comic and tragic in his hopeless love. He makes her think sometimes of a mouse singing amorous ballads under the window of a giantess.

"Good," she answers. "That's very good."

He nods again, as if they share a secret.

"But honestly," she says to her husband.

"Why should I wake you?" he answers. "Why shouldn't you sleep?"

"It's your *birth*day," she says.

"You need to rest."

He pats her belly carefully but with a certain force, as if it were the shell of a soft-boiled egg. Nothing shows yet; the only manifestations are a certain squeamishness and a subtle but distinct inner churning. She and her husband and son are in a house in which no one but they have ever lived. Outside the house is a world where the shelves are stocked, where radio waves are full of music, where young men walk the streets again, men who have known deprivation and a fear worse than death, who have willingly given up their early twenties and now, thinking of thirty and beyond, haven't any more time to spare. Their wartime training stands them in good stead. They are lean and strong. They are up at sunrise, uncomplaining.

"I like to make your breakfast," Laura says. "I feel fine."

"I can make breakfast. Just because I have to get up at the crack of dawn doesn't mean you have to."

"I want to."

The refrigerator hums. A bee thumps heavily, insistently, against a windowpane. Laura takes her pack of Pall Malls from the pocket of her robe. She is three years older than he (there is something vaguely disreputable about this, something vaguely embarrassing); a broad-shouldered woman, angular, dark, foreign-looking, although her family has been failing to prosper in this country for over a hundred years. She slides a cigarette out of the pack, changes her mind, slips it back in again.

"Okay," he says. "If you really want me to, tomorrow I'll wake you up at six."

"Okay."

She pours herself a cup of the coffee he's made. She comes back to him with the steaming cup in her hand, kisses his cheek. He pats her rump, affectionately and absentmindedly. He is no longer thinking of her. He is thinking about the day that lies ahead of him, the drive downtown, the torpid golden quiet of Wilshire Boulevard, where all the stores are still locked up and only the most cheerful and dedicated figures, young early-risers like himself, move through sunlight still innocent of the day's smog. His office will be silent, the typewriters in the secretarial pool still shrouded, and he and a few of the other men his age will have a full hour or more to get caught up on paperwork before the phones start ringing. It seems sometimes to be impossibly fine that he should have all this: an office and a new two-bedroom house, responsibilities and decisions, quick joking lunches with the other men.

"The roses are beautiful," Laura tells him. "How did you get them this early?"

"Mrs. Gar is in her shop at six. I just kept tapping at the glass until she let me in." He looks at his watch, though he knows what time it is. "Hey, I've got to go."

"Have a good day."

"You too."

"Happy birthday."

"Thank you."

He stands. For a while they are all absorbed in the ritual of his leaving: the taking on of jacket and briefcase; the flurry of kisses; the waves, he from over his shoulder as he crosses the lawn to the driveway, Laura and Richie from behind the screen door. Their lawn, extravagantly watered, is a brilliant, almost unearthly green. Laura and Richie stand like spectators at a parade as the man pilots his ice-blue Chevrolet down the short driveway and into the street. He waves one last time, jauntily, from behind the wheel.

"Well," she says, after the car has disappeared. Her son watches her adoringly, expectantly. She is the animating principle, the life of the house. Its rooms are sometimes larger than they should be; they sometimes, suddenly, contain things he's never seen before. He watches her, and waits.

"Well, now," she says.

Here, then, is the daily transition. With her husband present, she is more nervous but less afraid. She knows how to act. Alone with Richie, she sometimes feels unmoored—he is so entirely, persuasively himself. He wants what he wants so avidly. He cries mysteriously, makes indecipherable demands, courts her, pleads with her, ignores her. He seems, almost always, to be waiting to see what she will do next. She knows, or at least suspects, that other mothers of small children must maintain a body of rules and, more to the point, an ongoing mother-self to guide them in negotiating the days spent alone with a child. When her husband is here, she can manage it. She can see him seeing her, and she knows almost instinctively how to treat the boy firmly and kindly, with an affectionate maternal offhandedness that seems effortless. Alone with the child, though, she loses direction. She can't always remember how a mother would act.

"You need to finish your breakfast," she says to him.

"Okay," he says.

They return to the kitchen. Her husband has washed his coffee cup, dried it, put it away. The boy sets about eating with a certain tractorish steadiness that has more to do with obedience than appetite. Laura pours herself a fresh cup of coffee, sits at the table. She lights a cigarette.

. . . the triumph and the jingle and the strange high singing of some aeroplane overhead was what she loved; life; London; this moment of June.

She exhales a rich gray plume of smoke. She is so tired. She was up until after two, reading. She touches her belly—is it bad for the new baby, her getting so little sleep? She hasn't asked the doctor about it; she's afraid he'll tell her to stop reading altogether. She promises that tonight she'll read less. She'll go to sleep by midnight, at the latest.

She says to Richie, "Guess what we're going to do today? We're going to make a cake for your father's birthday. Oh, what a big job we have ahead of us."

He nods gravely, judiciously. He seems unconvinced about something.

She says, "We're going to make him the best cake he's ever seen. The very best. Don't you think that's a good idea?"

Again, Richie nods. He waits to see what will happen next.

Laura watches him through the meandering vine of cigarette smoke. She will not go upstairs, and return to her book. She will remain. She will do all that's required, and more.

Mrs. Dalloway

Clarissa carries her armload of flowers out into Spring Street. She imagines Barbara still in the cool dimness on the far side of the door, continuing to live in what Clarissa can't help thinking of now as the past (it has to do, somehow, with Barbara's sorrow, and the racks of ribbons on the back wall) while she herself walks into the present, all this: the Chinese boy careening by on a bicycle; the number 281 written in gold on dark glass; the scattering of pigeons with feet the color of pencil erasers (a bird had flown in through the open window of her fourth-grade classroom, violent, dreadful); Spring Street; and here she is with a huge bouquet of flowers. She will stop by Richard's apartment to see how he's doing (it's useless to call, he never answers), but first she goes and stands shyly, expectantly, not too close to the trailer from which the famous head emerged. A small crowd is gathered there, mostly tourists, and

Clarissa positions herself beside two young girls, one with hair dyed canary yellow and the other with hair dyed platinum. Clarissa wonders if they intended to so strongly suggest the sun and the moon.

Sun says to Moon, "It was Meryl Streep, definitely Meryl Streep."

Clarissa is excited, despite herself. She was right. There is a surprisingly potent satisfaction in knowing that her vision was shared by another.

"No way," says Moon. "It was Susan Sarandon."

It was not, Clarissa thinks, Susan Sarandon. It may have been Vanessa Redgrave but it was certainly not Susan Sarandon.

"No," says Sun, "it was Streep. Trust me."

"It was not Meryl Streep."

"It was. It fucking was."

Clarissa stands guiltily, holding her flowers, hoping the star will show herself again, embarrassed by her own interest. She is not given to fawning over celebrities, no more than most people, but can't help being drawn to the aura of fame—and more than fame, actual immortality—implied by the presence of a movie star in a trailer on the corner of MacDougal and Spring Streets. These two girls standing beside Clarissa, twenty if not younger, defiantly hefty, slouching into each other, laden with brightly colored bags from discount stores; these two girls will grow to middle and then old age, either wither or bloat; the cemeteries in which they're buried will fall eventually into ruin, the grass grown wild, browsed at night by dogs; and when all that remains of these girls is a few silver fillings lost underground the woman in the trailer, be she Meryl Streep or Vanessa Redgrave or even Susan Sarandon, will still be known. She will exist in archives, in books; her recorded voice will be stored away among other precious and venerated objects. Clarissa allows herself to continue standing, foolish as any fan, for another few minutes, in hope of seeing the star emerge. Yes, just another few minutes, before the humiliation is simply too much to bear. She remains before the trailer with her flowers. She watches the door. After several minutes have passed (nearly ten, although she hates admitting it) she leaves suddenly, indignantly, as if she's been stood up, and walks the few blocks uptown to Richard's apartment.

This neighborhood was once the center of something new and wild; something disreputable; a part of the city where the sound of guitars drifted all night out of bars and coffeehouses; where the stores that sold books and clothing smelled the way she imagined Arab bazaars must smell: incense and rich, dung-y dust, some sort of wood (cedar? camphor?), something fruitily, fertilely rotting; and where it had seemed possible, quite possible, that if you passed through the wrong door or down the wrong alley you would meet a fate: not just the familiar threat of robbery and physical harm but something more perverse and transforming, more permanent. Here, right here, on this corner, she had stood with Richard when Richard was nineteen—when Richard was a firm-featured, hard-eyed, not-quite-beautiful dark-haired boy with an impossibly long and graceful, very pale neck—here they had stood and argued . . . about what? A kiss? Had Richard kissed her, or had she, Clarissa, only believed Richard was about to kiss her, and evaded it? Here on this corner (in front of what had been a head shop and is now a delicatessen) they had kissed or not kissed, they had certainly argued, and here or somewhere soon after, they had canceled their little experiment, for Clarissa wanted her freedom and Richard wanted, well, too much, didn't he always? He wanted too much. She'd told him that what happened over the summer had been exactly that, something that happened over a summer. Why should he want her, a wry and diffident girl, no breasts to speak of (how could she be expected to trust his desire?), when he knew as well as she the bent of his deepest longings and when he had Louis, worshipful Louis, heavy-limbed, far from stupid, a boy Michelangelo would have been pleased to draw? Wasn't it, really, just another poetic conceit, Richard's idea of her? They had not had a large or spectacular fight, just a squabble on a corner—there had been no question, even then, of deep damage to the friendship—and yet as she looks back it seems definitive; it seems like the moment at which one possible future ended and a new one began. That day, after the argument (or possibly before it), Clarissa had bought a packet of incense and a gray alpaca jacket, secondhand, with rose-shaped buttons carved out of bone. Richard had eventually gone off to Europe with Louis. What, Clarissa wonders now, ever became of the alpaca jacket? It seems that she had it for years and years, and then suddenly didn't have it anymore.

She turns down Bleecker, goes up Thompson. The neighborhood today is an imitation of itself, a watered-down carnival for tourists, and Clarissa, at fifty-two, knows that behind these doors and down these alleys lies nothing more or less than people living their lives. Grotesquely, some of the same bars and coffeehouses are still here, done up now to resemble themselves for the benefit of Germans and Japanese. The stores all sell essentially the same things: souvenir T-shirts, cheap silver jewelry, cheap leather jackets.

At Richard's building she lets herself in through the vestibule door and thinks, as she always does, of the word "squalid." It is almost funny, the way the entrance to Richard's building so perfectly demonstrates the concept of squalor. It is so obviously, dreadfully squalid that it still surprises her slightly, even after all these years. It surprises her in almost the way a rare and remarkable object, a work of art, can continue to surprise; simply because it remains, throughout time, so purely and utterly itself. Here again, surprisingly, are the faded yellow-beige walls, more or less the color of an arrowroot biscuit; here is the fluorescent panel on the ceiling emitting its sputtering, watery glare. It is worse—much worse—that the cramped little lobby was cheaply and halfheartedly renovated a decade ago. The lobby is far more discouraging with its soiled white brick-patterned linoleum and its artificial ficus tree than it could possibly have been in its original decrepitude. Only the ancient marble wainscoting—a palomino-colored marble, veined in blue and gray with a deep yellow, smoky overlay, like a very fine old cheese, now hideously echoed by the yellowish walls—indicates that this was once a building of some consequence; that hopes were nurtured here; that upon entering the lobby people were expected to feel as if they were moving in an orderly fashion into a future that held something worth having.

She gets into the elevator, a tiny chamber of intensified, bleached brightness, paneled in wood-grain metal, and pushes the button for the fifth floor. The elevator door sighs and rattles shut. Nothing happens. Of course. It works only intermittently; in fact, it is something of a relief to abandon it and climb the stairs instead. Clarissa presses the button marked with a chipped white "O" and, after a nervous hesitation, the door rattles open again. She is always afraid of getting trapped between floors in this elevator—she can all too easily imagine the long, long wait; the cries for help to tenants who might or might not speak English and who might or might not care to intervene; the strange numbing deathlike fear of standing there, alone, for a considerable time, in the brilliant, stale-smelling emptiness, either looking or not looking at her distorted reflection in the dim circular mirror fastened to the upper right-hand corner. It is better, really, to find the elevator frankly inoperable, and to walk up five flights. It is better to be free.

She mounts the stairs, feeling both weary and bridal—virginal—with her armload of flowers. The treads of the stairs, chipped, worn down at their centers, are made of a peculiar, milky-black, rubberish substance. At each of the four landings a window offers a different view of laundry hanging from lines: flowered sheets, baby clothes, sweatpants; lurid in their inexpensive newness; not at all the sort of old-fashioned laundry—dark socks and elaborate women's underwear, faded housedresses, luminous white shirts—that would make the air shaft feel like something ordinary but marvelous, preserved from another time. Squalid, she thinks again. Simply, squalid.

Richard's hallway, painted the same arrowroot-biscuit color, is still tiled as it must have been at the turn of the century (the linoleum gives out, mysteriously, on the second story); its floor, bordered in a mosaic of geometric, pale-yellow flowers, bears a single cigarette butt stained with red lipstick. Clarissa knocks at Richard's door, pauses, knocks again.

"Who is it?"

"Just me."

"Who?"

"Clarissa."

"Oh, Mrs. D. Oh, come in."

Isn't it time, she thinks, to dispense with the old nickname? If he's having a good enough day, she'll bring it up: Richard, don't you think it's time to just call me Clarissa?

She opens the door with her key. She can hear Richard speaking in the other room, in a low, amused voice, as if he is imparting scandalous secrets. She can't tell what he is saying—she makes out the word "hurl," which is followed by Richard's low, rumbling laugh, a slightly pained sound, as if laughter were something sharp that had caught in his throat.

Well, Clarissa thinks, it's another day of this, then—not a day, certainly, to bring up the subject of names.

How can she help resenting Evan and all the others who got the new drugs in time; all the fortunate ("fortunate" being, of course, a relative term) men and women whose minds had not yet been eaten into lace by the virus. How can she help feeling angry on behalf of Richard, whose muscles and organs have been revived by the new discoveries but whose mind seems to have passed beyond any sort of repair other than the conferring of good days among the bad.

His apartment is, as always, dim and close, overheated, full of the sage and juniper incense Richard burns to cover the smells of illness. It is unutterably cluttered, inhabited here and there by a wan circle of pulverized non-dark emanating from the brown-shaded lamps in which Richard will tolerate no bulb more powerful than fifteen watts. The apartment has, more than anything, an underwater aspect. Clarissa walks through it as she would negotiate the hold of a sunken ship. It would not be entirely surprising if a small school of silver fish darted by in the half-light. These rooms do not seem, in any serious way, to be part of the building in which they happen to occur, and when Clarissa enters and closes behind her the big, creaky door with the four locks (two of them broken) she feels, always, as if she has passed through a dimensional warp—through the looking glass, as it were; as if the lobby, stairwell, and hallway exist in another realm altogether; another time.

"Good morning," she calls.

"Is it still morning?"

"Yes. It is."

Richard is in the second room. The apartment contains only two rooms: the kitchen (into which one enters) and the large other room, where Richard's life (what remains of it) is conducted. Clarissa passes through the kitchen, with its ancient stove and large white bathtub (dimly luminous as marble in the room's eternal dusk), its faint odor of gas and old cooking, its piled-up cardboard cartons full of . . . who knows what?, its gilt-framed oval mirror that gives back (always a bit of a shock, no matter how thoroughly expected) her pale reflection. Over the years, she has gotten used to ignoring the mirror.

Here is the Italian coffeemaker she bought for him, all chrome and black steel, beginning to join the general aspect of dusty disuse. Here are the copper pans she bought.

Richard, in the other room, sits in his chair. The shades are drawn and all six or seven lamps are lit, though their feeble output barely adds up to the illuminating power of one ordinary desk lamp. Richard, in the far corner, in his absurd flannel robe (an adult-size version of a child's robe, ink-blue, covered with rockets and helmeted astronauts), is as gaunt and majestic, and as foolish, as a drowned queen still seated on her throne.

He has stopped whispering. He sits with his head thrown back slightly and his eyes closed, as if listening to music.

"Good morning, my dear," Clarissa says again.

He opens his eyes. "Look at all those flowers."

"They're for you."

"Have I died?"

"They're for the party. How's your headache this morning?"

"Better. Thank you."

"Did you sleep?"

"I don't remember. Yes. I believe I did. Thank you."

"Richard, it's a beautiful summer day. How about if I let in a little light?"

"If you like."

She goes to the nearest of the three windows and, with some difficulty, raises the oiled-canvas shade. A compromised daylight—that which angles down between Richard's building and its chocolate-brick sister fifteen feet away—falls into the room. Across the alley is the window of a peevish old widow, with its glass and ceramic figures on the windowsill (a donkey pulling a cart, a clown, a grinning squirrel) and its venetian blinds. Clarissa turns. Richard's face, its hollows and deep, fleshly folds, its high glossy forehead and smashed pugilist's nose, seems to rise up out of the darkness like a sunken sculpture hauled to the surface.

"Awfully bright," he says.

"Light is good for you."

She goes to him, kisses the curve of his forehead. Up close like this, she can smell his various humors. His pores exude not only his familiar sweat (which has always smelled good to her, starchy and fermented; sharp in the way of wine) but the smell of his medicines, a powdery, sweetish smell. He smells, too, of unfresh flannel (though the laundry is done once a week, or oftener) and slightly, horribly (it is his only repellent smell), of the chair in which he spends his days.

Richard's chair, particularly, is insane; or, rather, it is the chair of someone who, if not actually insane, has let things slide so far, has gone such a long way toward the exhausted relinquishment of ordinary caretaking—simple hygiene, regular nourishment—that the difference between insanity and hopelessness is difficult to pinpoint. The chair—an elderly, square, overstuffed armchair obesely balanced on slender blond wooden legs—is ostentatiously broken and worthless. It is upholstered in something nubbly, no-colored, woolen, shot through (this is, somehow, its most sinister aspect) with silver thread. Its square arms and back are so worn down, so darkened by the continual application of friction and human oils, that they resemble the tender parts of an elephant's hide. Its coils are visible—perfect rows of pale, rusty rings—not only through the cushion of the seat but through the thin yellow towel Richard has draped over the cushion. The chair smells fetid and deeply damp, unclean; it smells of irreversible rot. If it were hauled out into the street (*when* it is hauled out into the street), no one would pick it up. Richard will not hear of its being replaced.

"Are they here today?" Clarissa asks.

"No," Richard answers, with the reluctant candor of a child. "They're gone now. They're very beautiful and quite terrible."

"Yes," she says. "I know."

"I think of them as coalescences of black fire, I mean they're dark and bright at the same time. There was one that looked a bit like a black, electrified jellyfish. They were singing, just now, in a foreign language. I believe it may have been Greek. Archaic Greek."

"Are you afraid of them?"

"No. Well, sometimes."

"I think I'm going to talk to Bing about increasing your medication, would that be all right?"

He sighs wearily. "The fact that I sometimes don't hear them or see them doesn't mean they're gone," he says.

"But if you don't hear them or see them," Clarissa says, "you can rest. Honestly, you didn't sleep at all last night, did you?"

"Oh, a little. I'm not so worried about sleep. I'm much more worried about you. You look so thin today, how *are* you?"

"*I'm* fine. I can only stay a minute. I've got to get the flowers in water."

"Right, right. The flowers, the party. Oh, my."

"I saw a movie star on my way over here," Clarissa says. "I think that's probably a good omen, don't you?"

Richard smiles wistfully. "Oh, well, omens," he says. "Do you believe in omens? Do you think we're taken that much notice of? Do you think we're worried over like that? My, wouldn't that be wonderful? Well, maybe it's so."

He will not ask the name of the movie star; he actually does not care. Richard, alone among Clarissa's acquaintance, has no essential interest in famous people. Richard genuinely does not recognize such distinctions. It is, Clarissa thinks, some combination of monumental ego and a kind of savantism. Richard cannot imagine a life more interesting or worthwhile than those being lived by his acquaintances and himself, and for that reason one often feels exalted, expanded, in his presence. He is not one of those egotists who miniaturize others. He is the opposite kind of egotist, driven by grandiosity rather than greed, and if he insists on a version of you that is funnier, stranger, more eccentric and profound than you suspect yourself to be—capable of doing more good and more harm in the world than you've ever imagined—it is all but impossible not to believe, at least in his presence and for a while after you've left him, that he alone sees through to your essence, weighs your true qualities (not all of which are necessarily flattering—a certain clumsy, childish rudeness is part of his style), and appreciates you more fully than anyone else ever has. It is only after knowing him for some time that you begin to realize you are, to him, an essentially fictional character, one he has invested with nearly limitless capacities for tragedy and comedy not because that is your true nature but because he, Richard, needs to live in a world peopled by extreme and commanding figures. Some have ended their relations with him rather than continue as figures in the epic poem he is always composing inside his head, the story of his life and passions; but others (Clarissa among them) enjoy the sense of hyperbole he brings to their lives, have come even to depend on it, the way they depend on coffee to wake them up in the mornings and a drink or two to send them off at night.

Clarissa says, "Superstitions are a comfort sometimes, I don't know why you so adamantly refuse all comforts."

"Do I? Oh, I don't mean to. I like comforts. Some of them. I like some of them very much."

"How *are* you feeling?"

"Well. Quite well. A bit ephemeral. I keep dreaming that I'm sitting in a room."

"The party's at five, do you remember? The party's at five, and the ceremony comes after, at eight, uptown. You remember all that, don't you?"

He says, "Yes."

Then he says, "No."

"Which is it?" she asks.

"Sorry. I seem to keep thinking things have already happened. When you asked if I remembered about the party and the ceremony, I thought you meant, did I remember having gone to them. And I did remember. I seem to have fallen out of time."

"The party and ceremony are tonight. In the future."

"I understand. In a way, I understand. But, you see, I seem to have gone into the future, too. I have a distinct recollection of the party that hasn't happened yet. I remember the award ceremony perfectly."

"Did they bring your breakfast this morning?" she asks.

"What a question. They did."

"And did you eat it?"

"I remember eating it. But it's possible that I only meant to. Is there a breakfast lying around here somewhere?"

"Not as far as I can see."

"Then I suppose I managed to eat it. Food doesn't matter much, does it?"

"Food matters a great deal, Richard."

He says, "I don't know if I can bear it, Clarissa."

"Bear what?"

"Being proud and brave in front of everybody. I recall it vividly. There I am, a sick, crazy wreck reaching out with trembling hands to receive his little trophy."

"Honey, you don't need to be proud. You don't need to be brave. It's not a performance."

"Of course it is. I got a prize for my performance, you must know that. I got a prize for having AIDS and going nuts and being brave about it, it had nothing to do with my work."

"Stop this. Please. It has everything to do with your work."

Richard draws and exhales a moist, powerful breath. Clarissa thinks of his lungs, glistening red pillows intricately embroidered with veins. They are, perversely, among his least compromised organs—for unknowable reasons, they have remained essentially unharmed by the virus. With that potent breath his eyes seem to focus, to gain greener depths.

"You don't think they'd give it to me if I were healthy, do you?" he says.

"Why, yes, as a matter of fact, I do."

"Please."

"Well, then, maybe you should refuse it."

"That's the awful thing," Richard says. "I want the prize. I do. It would be far easier if one cared either more or less about winning prizes. Is it here somewhere?"

"What?"

"The prize. I'd like to look at it."

"You haven't gotten it yet. It's tonight."

"Yes. That's right. Tonight."

"Richard, dear, listen to me. This can be simple. You can take simple, straightforward pleasure in this. I'll be there with you, every minute."

"I'd like that."

"It's a party. It's only a party. It will be populated entirely by people who respect and admire you."

"Really? Who?"

"You know who. Howard. Elisa. Martin Campo."

"Martin Campo? Oh, my lord."

"I thought you liked him. You've always said you did."

"Oh, well, yes, I suppose the lion likes the zookeeper, too."

"Martin Campo has steadfastly published you for over thirty years."

"Who else is coming?"

"We've been over and over this. You know who's coming."

"Tell me one more name, won't you? Tell me the name of someone heroic."

"Martin Campo is heroic, don't you think? He's sunk his entire family fortune into publishing important, difficult books he knows won't sell."

Richard closes his eyes, leans his gaunt head back against the worn, oily nubble of the chair. "All right, then," he says.

"You don't need to charm or entertain. You don't need to put in a performance. These people have believed in you for a long, long while. All you have to do is appear, sit on the sofa with or without a drink in your hand, listen or not listen, smile or not smile. That's it. I'll watch out for you."

She would like to take him by his bony shoulders and shake him, hard. Richard may (although one hesitates to think in quite these terms) be entering the canon; he may at these last moments in his earthly career be receiving the first hints of a recognition that will travel far into the future (assuming, of course, there is any future at all). A prize like this means more than the notice of a congress of poets and academics; it means that literature itself (the future of which is being shaped right now) seems to feel a need for Richard's particular contribution:

his defiantly prolix lamentations over worlds either vanishing or lost entirely. While there are no guarantees, it does seem possible, and perhaps even better than possible, that Clarissa and the small body of others have been right all along. Richard the dense, the wistful, the scrutinizing, Richard who observed so minutely and exhaustively, who tried to split the atom with words, will survive after other, more fashionable names have faded.

And Clarissa, Richard's oldest friend, his first reader—Clarissa who sees him every day, when even some of his more recent friends have come to imagine he's already died—is throwing him a party. Clarissa is filling her home with flowers and candles. Why shouldn't she want him to come?

Richard says, "I'm not really needed there, am I? The party can go on just with the idea of me. The party has already happened, really, with or without me."

"Now you're being impossible. I'm going to lose my patience soon."

"No, please, don't be angry. Oh, Mrs. D., the truth is, I'm embarrassed to go to this party. I've failed so terribly."

"Don't talk like that."

"No, no. You're kind, you're very kind, but I'm afraid I failed, and that's that. It was just too much for me. I thought I was a bigger figure than I was. Can I tell you an embarrassing secret? Something I've never told anyone?"

"Of course you can."

"I thought I was a genius. I actually used that word, privately, to myself."

"Well—"

"Oh, pride, pride. I was so wrong. It defeated me. It simply proved insurmountable. There was so much, oh, far too much for me. I mean, there's the weather, there's the water and the land, there are the animals, and the buildings, and the past and the future, there's space, there's history. There's this thread or something caught between my teeth, there's the old woman across the way, did you notice she switched the donkey and the squirrel on her windowsill? And, of course, there's time. And place. And there's you, Mrs. D. I wanted to tell part of the story of part of you. Oh, I'd love to have done that."

"Richard. You wrote a whole book."

"But everything's left out of it, almost everything. And then I just stuck on a shock ending. Oh, now, I'm not looking for sympathy, really. We want so much, don't we?"

"Yes. I suppose we do."

"You kissed me beside a pond."

"Ten thousand years ago."

"It's still happening."

"In a sense, yes."

"In reality. It's happening in that present. This is happening in this present."

"You're tired, darling. You must rest. I'm going to call Bing about your medicine, all right?"

"Oh, I can't, I can't rest. Come here, come closer, would you, please?"

"I'm right here."

"Closer. Take my hand."

Clarissa takes one of Richard's hands in hers. She is surprised, even now, at how frail it is—how palpably it resembles a bundle of twigs.

He says, "Here we are. Don't you think?"

"Pardon me?"

"We're middle-aged and we're young lovers standing beside a pond. We're everything, all at once. Isn't it remarkable?"

"Yes."

"I don't have any regrets, really, except that one. I wanted to write about you, about us, really. Do you know what I mean? I wanted to write about everything, the life we're having and the lives we might have had. I wanted to write about all the ways we might die."

"Don't regret anything, Richard," Clarissa says. "There's no need, you've done so much."

"It's kind of you to say so."

"What you need right now is a nap."

"Do you think so?"

"I do."

"All right, then."

She says, "I'll come to help you get dressed. How's three-thirty?"

"It's always wonderful to see you, Mrs. Dalloway."

"I'm going to go now. I've got to get the flowers in water."

"Yes. My, yes."

She touches his thin shoulder with her fingertips. How is it possible that she feels regret? How can she imagine, even now, that they might have had a life together? They might have been husband and wife, soul mates, with lovers on the side. There are ways of managing.

Richard was once avid and tall, sinewy, bright and pale as milk. He once strode through New York in an old military coat, talking excitedly, with the dark tangle of his hair tied impatiently away from his face by a length of blue ribbon he'd found.

Clarissa says, "I've made the crab thing. Not that I imagine that's any kind of serious inducement."

"Oh, you know how I love the crab thing. It does make a difference, of course it does. Clarissa?"

"Yes?"

He lifts his massive, ravaged head. Clarissa turns her face sideways, and receives Richard's kiss on her cheek. It's not a good idea to kiss him on the lips—a common cold would be a disaster for him. Clarissa receives the kiss on her cheek, squeezes Richard's thin shoulder with her fingertips.

"I'll see you at three-thirty," she says.

"Wonderful," Richard says. "Wonderful."

Mrs. Woolf

She looks at the clock on the table. Almost two hours have passed. She still feels powerful, though she knows that tomorrow she may look back at what she's written and find it airy, overblown. One always has a better book in one's mind than one can manage to get onto paper. She takes a sip of cold coffee, and allows herself to read what she's written so far.

It seems good enough; parts seem very good indeed. She has lavish hopes, of course—she wants this to be her best book, the one that finally matches her expectations. But can a single day in the life of an ordinary woman be made into enough for a novel? Virginia taps at her lips with her thumb. Clarissa Dalloway will die, of that she feels certain, though this early it's impossible to say how or even precisely why. She will, Virginia believes, take her own life. Yes, she will do that.

Virginia lays down her pen. She would like to write all day, to fill thirty pages instead of three, but after the first hours something within her falters, and she worries that if she pushes beyond her limits she will taint the whole enterprise. She will let it wander into a realm of incoherence from which it might never return. At the same time, she hates spending any of her cogent hours doing anything but writing. She works, always, against the fear of relapse. First come the headaches, which are not in any way ordinary pain ("headache" has always seemed an inadequate term for them, but to call them by any other would be too melodramatic). They infiltrate her. They inhabit rather than merely afflict her, the way viruses inhabit their hosts. Strands of pain announce themselves, throw shivers of brightness into her eyes so insistently she must remind herself that others can't see them. Pain colonizes her, quickly replaces what was Virginia with more and more of itself, and its advance is so forceful, its jagged contours so distinct, that she can't help imagining it as an entity with a life of its own. She might see it while walking with Leonard in the square, a scintillating silver-white mass floating over the cobblestones, randomly spiked, fluid but whole, like a jellyfish. "What's that?" Leonard would ask. "It's my headache," she'd answer. "Please ignore it."

The headache is always there, waiting, and her periods of freedom, however long, always feel provisional. Sometimes the headache simply takes partial possession for an evening or a day or two, then withdraws. Sometimes it remains and increases until she herself subsides. At those times the headache moves out of her skull and into the world. Everything glows and pulses. Everything is infected with brightness, throbbing with it, and she prays for dark the way a wanderer lost in the desert prays for water. The world is every bit as barren of darkness as a desert is of water. There is no dark in the shuttered room, no dark behind her eyelids. There are only greater and lesser degrees of radiance. When she's crossed over to this realm of relentless brilliance, the voices start. Sometimes they are low, disembodied grumblings that coalesce out of the air itself; sometimes they emanate from behind the furniture or inside the walls. They are indistinct but full of meaning, undeniably masculine, obscenely old. They are angry, accusatory, disillusioned. They seem sometimes to be conversing, in whispers, among themselves; they seem sometimes to be reciting text. Sometimes, faintly, she can distinguish a word. "Hurl," once, and "under" on two occasions. A flock of sparrows outside her window once sang, unmistakably, in Greek. This state makes her hellishly miserable; in this state she is capable of shrieking at Leonard or anyone else who comes near (fizzling, like devils, with light); and yet this state when protracted also begins to enshroud her, hour by hour, like a chrysalis. Eventually, when enough hours have passed, she emerges bloodied, trembling, but full of vision and ready, once she's rested, to work again. She dreads her lapses into pain and light and she suspects they are necessary. She has been free for quite some time now, for years. She knows how suddenly the headache can return but she discounts it in Leonard's presence, acts more firmly healthy than she sometimes feels. She will return to London. Better to die raving mad in London than evaporate in Richmond.

She decides, with misgivings, that she is finished for today. Always, there are these doubts. Should she try another hour? Is she being judicious, or slothful? Judicious, she tells herself, and almost believes it. She has her two hundred and fifty words, more or less. Let it be enough. Have faith that you will be here, recognizable to yourself, again tomorrow.

She takes her cup, with its cold dregs, and walks out of the room and down the stairs to the printing room, where Ralph is reading the page proofs as Leonard finishes with them.

"Good morning," Ralph says brightly and nervously to Virginia. His broad, placid, handsome face is red, his forehead practically aglow, and she can immediately see that, for him, it is not a good morning at all. Leonard must have growled at some inefficiency, either of recent vintage or left over from yesterday, and now Ralph sits reading proofs and saying "Good morning" with the flushed ardency of a scolded child.

"Good morning," she answers, in a voice that is cordial but carefully unsympathetic. These young men and women, these assistants, will come and go; already Marjorie has been hired (with her terrible drawl, and where is she just now?) to do the jobs Ralph considers beneath him. It won't be long, surely, before Ralph and then Marjorie have gone on and she, Virginia, emerges from her study to find someone new wishing her a red-faced, chastened good morning. She knows Leonard can be gruff, stingy, and all but impossibly demanding. She knows these young people are often criticized unfairly but she will not side with them against him. She will not be the mother who intervenes, much as they beg her to with their eager smiles and wounded eyes. Ralph, after all, is Lytton's worry, and Lytton is welcome to him. He, like his brothers or sisters to come, will go on and do whatever they do in the greater world—no one expects them to make a career out of assisting at the press. Leonard may be autocratic, he may be unfair, but he is her companion and caretaker, and she will not betray him, certainly not for handsome, callow Ralph, or Marjorie, with her parakeet's voice.

"There are ten errors in eight pages," Leonard says. The brackets around his mouth are so deep you could slip a penny in.

"Lucky to have found them," Virginia says.

"They seem to congregate around the middle section. Do you think bad writing actually attracts a higher incidence of misfortune?"

"How I'd love to live in a world in which that were true. I'm going for a walk to clear my head, then I'll come and pitch in."

"We're making good progress," Ralph says. "We should be through by the end of the day."

"We shall be lucky," Leonard says, "to be through by this time next week."

He glowers; Ralph turns a finer and more precise shade of red. Of course, she thinks. Ralph set the type, and did it carelessly. The truth, she thinks, sits calmly and plumply, dressed in matronly gray, between these two men. It does not reside with Ralph, the young foot soldier, who appreciates literature but appreciates also, with equal or perhaps greater fervor, the brandy and biscuits waiting when the day's work is done; who is good-hearted and unexceptional and can barely be counted on to perpetuate, in his allotted span, the ordinary business of the ordinary world. The truth likewise does not (alas) reside with Leonard, brilliant and indefatigable Leonard, who refuses to distinguish between setback and catastrophe; who worships accomplishment above all else and makes himself unbearable to others because he genuinely believes he can root out and reform every incidence of human fecklessness and mediocrity.

"I'm sure," she says, "that between us we can get the book into some sort of acceptable shape, and still have Christmas."

Ralph grins at her with a relief so visible she has an urge to slap him. He overestimates her sympathy—she has spoken not on his behalf but on Leonard's, in much the way her own mother might have made light of a servant's blunder during dinner, declaring for the sake of her husband and all others present that the shattered tureen portended nothing; that the circle of love and forbearance could not be broken; that all were safe.

Mrs. Brown

Life, London, this moment of June.

She begins sifting flour into a blue bowl. Outside the window is the brief interlude of grass that separates this house from the neighbors'; the shadow of a bird streaks across the blinding white stucco of the neighbors' garage. Laura is briefly, deeply pleased by the shadow of the bird, the bands of brilliant white and green. The bowl on the counter before her is a pale, chalky, slightly faded blue with a thin band of white leaves at the rim. The leaves are identical, stylized, slightly cartoonish, canted at rakish angles, and it seems perfect and inevitable that one of them has suffered a small, precisely triangular nick in its side. A fine white rain of flour falls into the bowl.

"There we are," she says to Richie. "Do you want to see?"

"Yes," he answers.

She kneels to show him the sifted flour. "Now. We have to

measure out four cups. Oh, my. Do you know how many four is?"

He holds up four fingers. "Good," she says. "Very good."

At this moment she could devour him, not ravenously but adoringly, infinitely gently, the way she used to take the Host into her mouth before she married and converted (her mother will never forgive her, never). She is full of a love so strong, so unambiguous, it resembles appetite.

"You're such a good, smart boy," she says.

Richie grins; he looks ardently into her face. She looks back at him. They pause, motionless, watching each other, and for a moment she is precisely what she appears to be: a pregnant woman kneeling in a kitchen with her three-year-old son, who knows the number four. She is herself and she is the perfect picture of herself; there is no difference. She is going to produce a birthday cake—only a cake—but in her mind at this moment the cake is glossy and resplendent as any photograph in any magazine; it is better, even, than the photographs of cakes in magazines. She imagines making, out of the humblest materials, a cake with all the balance and authority of an urn or a house. The cake will speak of bounty and delight the way a good house speaks of comfort and safety. This, she thinks, is how artists or architects must feel (it's an awfully grand comparison, she knows, maybe even a little foolish, but still), faced with canvas, with stone, with oil or wet cement. Wasn't a book like *Mrs. Dalloway* once just empty paper and a pot of ink? It's only a cake, she tells herself. But still. There are cakes and then there are cakes. At this moment, holding a bowl full of sifted flour in an orderly house under the California sky, she hopes to be as satisfied and as filled with anticipation as a writer putting down the first sentence, a builder beginning to draw the plans.

"Okeydoke," she says to Richie. "You do the first one."

She hands him a bright aluminum cup measure. It is the first time he's been entrusted with a job like this. Laura sets a second bowl, empty, on the floor for him. He holds the measuring cup in both hands.

"Here goes," she says.

Guiding Richie's hands with her own, she helps him dip the cup into the flour. The cup goes in easily, and through its thin wall he can feel the silkiness and slight grit of the sifted flour. A tiny cloud rises in the cup's wake. Mother and son bring it up again, heaped with flour. Flour cascades down the silver sides. Laura tells the boy to hold the cup steady, which he nervously manages to do, and with one quick gesture she dismisses the grainy little heap on top and creates a flawless white surface exactly level with the lip of the cup. He continues holding the cup with both hands.

"Good," she says. "Now we put it in the other bowl. Do you think you can do that by yourself?"

"Yes," he says, though he is not at all certain. He believes this cup of flour to be singular and irreplaceable. It is one thing to be asked to carry a cabbage across the street, quite another to be asked to carry the recently unearthed head of Rilke's Apollo.

"Here we go, then," she says.

He cautiously moves the cup to the other bowl and holds it there, paralyzed, over the bowl's gleaming white concavity (it is the next smaller in a series of nesting bowls, pale green, with the same band of white leaves at its rim). He understands that he's expected to dump the flour into the bowl but it seems possible that he's misunderstood the directions, and will ruin everything; it seems possible that by spilling out the flour he will cause some larger catastrophe, upset some precarious balance. He wants to look at his mother's face but can't take his eyes off the cup.

"Turn it over," she says.

He turns it over in one hurried, frightened motion. The flour hesitates for a fraction of a second, then spills out. The flour falls solidly, in a mound that loosely echoes the shape of the measuring cup. A bigger cloud rises, almost touches his face, then vanishes. He stares down at what he's made: a white hill, slightly granular, speckled with pinpoint shadows, standing up from the glossy, creamier white of the bowl's interior.

"Oopsie," his mother says.

He looks at her in terror. His eyes fill with tears.

Laura sighs. Why is he so delicate, so prone to fits of inexplicable remorse? Why does she have to be so careful with him? For a moment—a moment—Richie's shape subtly changes. He becomes larger, brighter. His head expands. A dead-white glow seems, briefly, to surround him. For a moment she wants only to leave—not to harm him, she'd never do that—but to be free, blameless, unaccountable.

"No, no," Laura says. "It's good. Very good. That's just exactly right."

He smiles tearfully, suddenly proud of himself, almost insanely relieved. All right, then; nothing was needed but a few kind words, a bit of reassurance. She sighs. She gently touches his hair.

"Now, then," she says. "Are you ready to do another one?"

He nods with such guileless, unguarded enthusiasm that her throat constricts in a spasm of love. It seems suddenly easy to bake a cake, to raise a child. She loves her son purely, as mothers do—she does not resent him, does not wish to leave. She loves her husband, and is glad to be married. It seems possible (it does not seem impossible) that she's slipped across an invisible line, the line that has always separated her from what she would prefer to feel, who she would prefer to be. It does not seem impossible that she has undergone a subtle but profound transformation, here in this kitchen, at this most ordinary of moments: She has caught up with herself. She has worked so long, so hard, in such good faith, and now she's gotten the knack of living happily, as herself, the way a child learns at a particular moment to balance on a two-wheel bicycle. It seems she will be fine. She will not lose hope. She will not mourn her lost possibilities, her unexplored talents (what if she has no talents, after all?). She will remain devoted to her son, her husband, her home and duties, all her gifts. She will want this second child.

Mrs. Woolf

She walks up Mt. Ararat Road, planning Clarissa Dalloway's suicide. Clarissa will have had a love: a woman. Or a girl, rather; yes, a girl she knew during her own girlhood; one of those passions that flare up when one is young—when love and ideas seem truly to be one's personal discovery, never before apprehended in quite this way; during that brief period of youth when one feels free to do or say anything; to shock, to strike out; to refuse the future that's been offered and demand another, far grander and stranger, devised and owned wholly by oneself, owing nothing to old Aunt Helena, who sits every night in her accustomed chair and wonders aloud whether Plato and Morris are suitable reading for young women. Clarissa Dalloway, in her first youth, will love another girl, Virginia thinks; Clarissa will believe that a rich, riotous future is opening before her, but eventually (how, exactly, will the change be accomplished?) she will come to her senses, as young women do, and marry a suitable man.

Yes, she will come to her senses, and marry.

She will die in middle age. She will kill herself, probably, over some trifle (how can it be made convincing, tragic instead of comic?).

That, of course, will occur later in the book, and by the time Virginia reaches that destination she hopes its precise nature will have revealed itself. For now, walking through Richmond, she focuses her thoughts on the question of Clarissa's first love. A girl. The girl, she thinks, will be brash and captivating. She will scandalize the aunts by cutting the heads off dahlias and hollyhocks and floating them in great bowls of water, just as Virginia's sister, Vanessa, has always done.

Here on Mt. Ararat Road Virginia passes a stout woman, a familiar figure from the shops, a hale and suspicious old wife who walks two pugs on brandy-colored leashes, who carries an immense tapestry handbag in her other hand, and who, by her ostentatious ignoring of Virginia, clearly indicates that Virginia has, again, been talking aloud without quite realizing it. Yes, she can practically hear her own muttered words, *scandalize the aunts*, still streaming like a scarf behind her. Well, what of it? Brazenly, after the woman has passed, Virginia turns, fully prepared to stare down the woman's surreptitious glance backward. Virginia's eyes meet those of one of the pugs, which stares over its fawn-colored shoulder at her with an expression of moist, wheezing bafflement.

She reaches Queen's Road and turns back toward home,

thinking of Vanessa, of decapitated flowers floating in bowls of water.

Although it is among the best of them, Richmond is, finally and undeniably, a suburb, only that, with all the word implies about window boxes and hedges; about wives walking pugs; about clocks striking the hours in empty rooms. Virginia thinks of the love of a girl. She despises Richmond. She is starved for London; she dreams sometimes about the hearts of cities. Here, where she has been taken to live for the last eight years precisely because it is neither strange nor marvelous, she is largely free of the headaches and voices, the fits of rage. Here all she desires is a return to the dangers of city life.

On the steps of Hogarth House, she pauses to remember herself. She has learned over the years that sanity involves a certain measure of impersonation, not simply for the benefit of husband and servants but for the sake, first and foremost, of one's own convictions. She is the author; Leonard, Nelly, Ralph, and the others are the readers. This particular novel concerns a serene, intelligent woman of painfully susceptible sensibilities who once was ill but has now recovered; who is preparing for the season in London, where she will give and attend parties, write in the mornings and read in the afternoons, lunch with friends, dress perfectly. There is true art in it, this command of tea and dinner tables; this animating correctness. Men may congratulate themselves for writing truly and passionately about the movements of nations; they may consider war and the search for God to be great literature's only subjects; but if men's standing in the world could be toppled by an ill-advised choice of hat, English literature would be dramatically changed.

Clarissa Dalloway, she thinks, will kill herself over something that seems, on the surface, like very little. Her party will fail, or her husband will once again refuse to notice some effort she's made about her person or their home. The trick will be to render intact the magnitude of Clarissa's miniature but very real desperation; to fully convince the reader that, for her, domestic defeats are every bit as devastating as are lost battles to a general.

Virginia walks through the door. She feels fully in command of the character who is Virginia Woolf, and as that character she removes her cloak, hangs it up, and goes downstairs to the kitchen to speak to Nelly about lunch.

In the kitchen, Nelly is rolling out a crust. Nelly is herself, always herself; always large and red, regal, indignant, as if she'd spent her life in an age of glory and decorum that ended, forever, some ten minutes before you entered the room. Virginia marvels at her. How does she remember, how does she manage, every day and every hour, to be so exactly the same?

"Hello, Nelly," Virginia says.

"Hello, ma'am." Nelly concentrates on the crust, as if her rolling pin were revealing faint but legible writing in the dough.

"Is that a pie for lunch?"

"Yes, ma'am. I thought a lamb pie, there's that lamb left over, and you was so hard at work this morning we didn't speak."

"A lamb pie sounds lovely," Virginia says, though she must work to stay in character. She reminds herself: food is not sinister. Do not think of putrefaction or feces; do not think of the face in the mirror.

"I've got the cress soup," Nelly says. "And the pie. And then I thought just some of them yellow pears for pudding, unless you'd like something fancier."

Here it is, then: the challenge thrown down. *Unless you'd like something fancier.* So the subjugated Amazon stands on the riverbank wrapped in the fur of animals she has killed and skinned; so she drops a pear before the queen's gold slippers and says, "Here is what I've brought. Unless you'd like something fancier."

"Pears will be fine," Virginia says, though of course pears will not be fine at all; not now. If Virginia had performed properly and appeared in the kitchen that morning to order lunch, the pudding could be almost anything. It could be blancmange or a soufflé; it could, in fact, be pears. Virginia could easily have walked into the kitchen at eight o'clock and said, "Let's not bother much about the pudding today, pears will suit us perfectly." But instead she skulked straightaway to her study, fearful that her day's writing (that fragile impulse, that egg balanced on a spoon) might dissolve before one of Nelly's moods. Nelly knows this, of course she knows, and in offering pears she reminds Virginia that she, Nelly, is powerful; that she knows secrets; that queens who care more about solving puzzles in their chambers than they do about the welfare of their people must take whatever they get.

Virginia picks up a curl of crust from the pastry board, molds it between her fingers. She says, "Do you remember that Vanessa and the children are coming at four?"

"Yes, ma'am, I remember." Nelly lifts the crust with elaborate competence and drapes it into the pie pan. The tender, practiced movement reminds Virginia of changing a baby's nappies and briefly she feels like a girl witnessing, in awe and fury, the impenetrable competence of a mother.

She says, "There should be China tea, I think. And sugared ginger."

"China tea, ma'am? And ginger?"

"We've not had Vanessa in more than a fortnight. I'd prefer to give her something better than yesterday's scraps for tea."

"China tea and sugared ginger would mean London, they don't sell that here."

"The trains run on the half hour, the buses on the hour. Aren't there other things we need in London?"

"Oh, there's always things. It's just, it's half past eleven now, and luncheon is far from finished. Missus Bell comes at four. You said four, didn't you?"

"Yes, and by four o'clock I meant the four o'clock that arrives almost five hours from now, now being exactly eight minutes past eleven. The twelve-thirty train would get you to London a few minutes past one. The two-thirty would deposit you back here just after three, quite promptly and safely, with the tea and ginger in hand. Am I miscalculating?"

"No," says Nelly. She takes a turnip from the bowl and cuts off its end with a practiced flick of the knife. So, Virginia thinks, she would like to slit my throat; just so, with an offhand stroke, as if killing me were another of the domestic chores that stand between her and sleep. That is how Nelly would murder, competently and precisely, the way she cooks, following recipes learned so long ago she does not experience them as knowledge at all. At this moment she would gladly cut Virginia's throat like a turnip because Virginia neglected her own duties and now she, Nelly Boxall, a grown woman, is being punished for serving pears. Why is it so difficult dealing with servants? Virginia's mother managed beautifully. Vanessa manages beautifully. Why is it so difficult to be firm and kind with Nelly; to command her respect and her love? Virginia knows just how she should enter the kitchen, how her shoulders should be set, how her voice should be motherly but not familiar, something like that of a governess speaking to a beloved child. *Oh, let's have something more than pears, Nelly, Mr. Woolf is in a mood today and I'm afraid pears won't do nearly enough to sweeten his disposition*. It should be so simple.

She will give Clarissa Dalloway great skill with servants, a manner that is intricately kind and commanding. Her servants will love her. They will do more than she asks.

Mrs. Dalloway

Entering the hallway with her flowers, Clarissa meets Sally on her way out. For a moment—less than a moment—she sees Sally as she would if they were strangers. Sally is a pale, gray-haired woman, harsh-faced, impatient, ten pounds lighter than she ought to be. For a moment, seeing this stranger in the hall, Clarissa is filled with tenderness and a vague, clinical disapproval. Clarissa thinks, She is so agitated and lovely. Clarissa thinks, She should never wear yellow, not even this deep mustard tone.

"Hey," Sally says. "Great flowers."

They kiss quickly, on the lips. They are always generous with kisses.

"Where are you going?" Clarissa asks.

"Uptown. Lunch with Oliver St. Ives. Did I tell you? I can't remember if I told you."

"You didn't."

"Sorry. Do you mind?"

"Not at all. Nice to be having lunch with a movie star."

"I cleaned like a demon in there."

"Toilet paper?"

"There's plenty. I'll be back in a couple of hours."

"Bye."

"The flowers are great," Sally says. "Why do I feel nervous?"

"Having lunch with a movie star, I suppose."

"It's just Oliver. I feel like I'm abandoning you."

"You're not. Everything's fine."

"You're sure?"

"Go. Have a good time."

"Bye."

They kiss again. Clarissa will speak to Sally, when the time seems right, about retiring the mustard-colored jacket.

As she continues down the hall, she wonders over the pleasure she felt—what had it been?—just a little more than an hour earlier. At this moment, at eleven-thirty on a warm June day, the hallway of her building feels like an entrance to the realm of the dead. The urn sits in its niche and the brown-glazed floor tiles silently return, in muddied form, the elderly ocher light of the sconces. No, not the realm of the dead, exactly; there is something worse than death, with its promise of release and slumber. There is dust rising, endless days, and a hallway that sits and sits, always full of the same brown light and the dank, slightly chemical smell that will do, until something more precise comes along, as the actual odor of age and loss, the end of hope. Richard, her lost lover, her truest friend, is disappearing into his illness, his insanity. Richard will not accompany her, as planned, into old age.

Clarissa lets herself into the apartment and immediately, oddly, feels better. A little better. There's the party to think about. At least there's that. Here is her home; hers and Sally's; and although they've lived here together almost fifteen years she is still struck by its beauty and by their impossible good fortune. Two floors and a garden in the West Village! They are rich, of course; obscenely rich by the world's standards; but not *rich* rich, not New York City rich. They had a certain amount to spend and they lucked into these pine-planked floors, this bank of casement windows that open onto the bricked patio where emerald moss grows in shallow stone troughs and a small circular fountain, a platter of clear water, burbles at the touch of a switch. Clarissa takes the flowers into the kitchen, where Sally has left a note ("Lunch w. Oliver—did I forget to tell U?—back by 3 latest, XXXXX"). Clarissa is filled, suddenly, with a sense of dislocation. This is not her kitchen at all. This is the kitchen of an acquaintance, pretty enough but not her taste, full of foreign smells. She lives elsewhere. She lives in a room where a tree gently taps against the glass as someone touches a needle to a phonograph record. Here in this kitchen white dishes are stacked pristinely, like holy implements, behind glassed cupboard doors. A row of old terra-cotta pots, glazed in various shades of crackled yellow, stand on the granite countertop. Clarissa recognizes these things but stands apart from them. She feels the presence of her own ghost; the part of her at once most indestructibly alive and least distinct; the part that owns nothing; that observes with wonder and detachment, like a tourist in a museum, a row of glazed yellow pots and a countertop with a single crumb on it, a chrome spigot from which a single droplet trembles, gathers weight, and falls. She and Sally bought all these things, she can remember every transaction, but she feels now that they are arbitrary, the spigot and the counter and the pots, the white dishes. They are only choices, one thing and then another, yes or no, and she sees how easily she could slip out of this life—these empty and arbitrary comforts. She could simply leave it and return to her other home, where neither Sally nor Richard exists; where there is only the essence of Clarissa, a girl grown into a woman, still full of hope, still capable of anything. It is revealed to her that all her sorrow and loneliness, the whole creaking scaffold of it, stems simply from pretending to live in this apartment among these objects, with kind, nervous Sally, and that if she leaves she'll be happy, or better than happy. She'll be herself. She feels briefly, wonderfully alone, with everything ahead of her.

Then the feeling moves on. It does not collapse; it is not whisked away. It simply moves on, like a train that stops at a small country station, stands for a while, and then continues out of sight. Clarissa pulls the flowers from their paper, puts them in the sink. She is disappointed and more than a little relieved. This is, in fact, her apartment, her collection of clay pots, her mate, her life. She wants no other. Feeling regular, neither elated nor depressed, simply present as Clarissa

Vaughan, a fortunate woman, professionally well regarded, giving a party for a celebrated and mortally ill artist, she goes back to the living room to check the messages on the answering machine. The party will go well or badly. Either way, she and Sally will have dinner afterward. They will go to bed.

On the tape is the new caterer (he has an untraceable accent; what if he's incompetent?) confirming his three o'clock delivery. There is a guest asking for permission to bring along a guest of her own, and another announcing that he has to leave town that morning to see a childhood friend whose AIDS has developed, unexpectedly, into leukemia.

The machine clicks off. Clarissa pushes the rewind button. If Sally forgot to mention her lunch with Oliver St. Ives it's probably because the invitation was made to Sally alone. Oliver St. Ives, the scandal, the hero, has not asked Clarissa to lunch. Oliver St. Ives, who came out spectacularly in *Vanity Fair* and was subsequently dropped from his leading role in an expensive thriller, has gained more notoriety as a gay activist than he could ever have hoped for had he continued posing as a heterosexual and cranking out pricey B-movies. Sally met Oliver St. Ives when he appeared on the very serious, very highbrow interview show she co-produces (which would never, of course, have considered him when he was just an action hero, and not one of the first rank). Sally has become someone he invites to lunch, though he and Clarissa have met several times by now and had what Clarissa recalls as a long and surprisingly intimate conversation at a fund-raiser. Doesn't it matter that she's the woman in the book? (Though the book, of course, failed, and though Oliver, of course, probably reads very little.) Oliver did not say to Sally, "Be sure to bring that interesting woman you live with." He probably thought Clarissa was a wife; only a wife. Clarissa returns to the kitchen. She isn't jealous of Sally, it isn't anything as cheap as that, but she cannot help feeling, in being passed over by Oliver St. Ives, the waning of the world's interest in her and, more powerfully, the embarrassing fact that it matters to her even now, as she prepares a party for a man who may be a great artist and may not survive the year. I am trivial, endlessly trivial, she thinks. And yet. Going uninvited feels in some way like a minor demonstration of the world's ability to get along without her. Being passed over by Oliver St. Ives (who probably did not consciously exclude her but simply did not think of her at all) resembles death the way a child's shoebox diorama of a historic event resembles the event itself. It's a tiny thing, bright, shabby, all felt and glue. But nevertheless. It isn't failure, she tells herself. It isn't failure to be in these rooms, in your skin, cutting the stems of flowers. It isn't failure but it requires more of you, the whole effort does; just being present and grateful; being happy (terrible word). People don't look at you on the street anymore, or if they do it is not with sexual notions of any sort. You are not invited to lunch by Oliver St. Ives. Outside the narrow kitchen window the city sails and rumbles. Lovers argue; cashiers ring up; young men and women shop for new clothes as the woman standing under the Washington Square Arch sings *iiiii* and you snip the end off a rose and put it in a vase full of hot water. You try to hold the moment, just here, in the kitchen with the flowers. You try to inhabit it, to love it, because it's yours and because what waits immediately outside these rooms is the hallway, with its brown tiles and its dim brown lamps that are always lit. Because even if the door to the trailer had opened, the woman inside, be she Meryl Streep or Vanessa Redgrave or even Susan Sarandon, would have been simply that, a woman in a trailer, and you could not possibly have done what you wanted to do. You could not have received her, there on the street; taken her in your arms; and wept with her. It would be so wonderful to cry like that, in the arms of a woman who was at once immortal and a tired, frightened person just emerged from a trailer. What you are, more than anything, is alive, right here in your kitchen, just as Meryl Streep and Vanessa Redgrave are alive somewhere, as traffic grumbles in from Sixth Avenue and the silver blades of the scissors cut juicily through a dark green stalk.

That summer when she was eighteen, it seemed anything could happen, anything at all. It seemed that she could kiss her grave, formidable best friend down by the pond, it seemed that they could sleep together in a strange combination of lust and innocence, and not worry about what, if anything, it meant. It was the house, really, she thinks. Without the house they would simply have remained three undergraduates who smoked joints and argued in the dormitories at Columbia. It was the house. It was the chain of events initiated by the old aunt and uncle's fatal congress with a produce truck on the outskirts of Plymouth, and Louis's parents offering him and his friends the use, for the whole summer, of the suddenly vacated house, where lettuce was still fresh in the refrigerator and a feral cat kept checking, with growing impatience, for the scraps it had always found outside the kitchen door. It was the house and the weather—the ecstatic unreality of it all—that helped turn Richard's friendship into a more devouring kind of love, and it was those same elements, really, that brought Clarissa here, to this kitchen in New York City, where she stands on Italian slate (a mistake, it's cold and subject to stains), cutting flowers and struggling, with only moderate success, to stop caring that Oliver St. Ives, the activist and ruined movie star, has not asked her to lunch.

It was not betrayal, she had insisted; it was simply an expansion of the possible. She did not require fidelity of Richard—god forbid!—and she was not in any way extorting property that belonged to Louis. Louis didn't think so, either (or at least wouldn't admit to thinking so, but really, could it have been mere chance that he cut himself so often that summer, with various tools and kitchen knives, and that he required two separate trips to the local doctor for stitches?). It was 1965; love spent might simply engender more of the same. It seemed possible, at least. Why not have sex with everybody, as long as you wanted them and they wanted you? So Richard continued with Louis and started up with her as well, and it felt right; simply right. Not that sex and love were uncomplicated. Clarissa's attempts with Louis, for instance, failed utterly. He was not interested in her nor she in him, for all his celebrated beauty. They both loved Richard, they both wanted Richard, and that would have to do as a bond between them. Not all people were meant to be lovers, and they were not naïve enough to try and force it beyond one stoned failure in the bed Louis would share, for the rest of the summer, only with Richard, on the nights Richard was not with Clarissa.

How often since then has she wondered what might have happened if she'd tried to remain with him; if she'd returned Richard's kiss on the corner of Bleecker and MacDougal, gone off somewhere (where?) with him, never bought the packet of incense or the alpaca coat with the rose-shaped buttons. Couldn't they have discovered something . . . larger and stranger than what they've got? It is impossible not to imagine that other future, that rejected future, as taking place in Italy or France, among big sunny rooms and gardens; as being full of infidelities and great battles; as a vast and enduring romance laid over friendship so searing and profound it would accompany them to the grave and possibly even beyond. She could, she thinks, have entered another world. She could have had a life as potent and dangerous as literature itself.

Or then again maybe not, Clarissa tells herself. That's who I was. That's who I am—a decent woman with a good apartment, with a stable and affectionate marriage, giving a party. Venture too far for love, she tells herself, and you renounce citizenship in the country you've made for yourself. You end up just sailing from port to port.

Still, there is this sense of missed opportunity. Maybe there is nothing, ever, that can equal the recollection of having been young together. Maybe it's as simple as that. Richard was the person Clarissa loved at her most optimistic moment. Richard had stood beside her at a pond's edge at dusk, wearing cut-off jeans and rubber sandals. Richard had called her Mrs. Dalloway, and they had kissed. His mouth had opened into hers; his tongue (exciting and utterly familiar, she'd never forget it) had worked its way shyly inside until she met it with her own. They'd kissed, and walked around the pond together. In another hour they'd have dinner, and considerable quantities of wine. Clarissa's copy of *The Golden Notebook* lay on the chipped white nightstand of the attic bedroom where she still slept alone; where Richard had not yet begun to spend alternate nights.

It had seemed like the beginning of happiness, and Clarissa is still sometimes shocked, more than thirty years later, to realize that it *was* happiness; that the entire experience lay in a kiss and a walk, the anticipation of dinner and a book. The dinner is by now forgotten; Lessing has been long overshadowed by other writers; and even the sex, once she and Richard reached that point, was ardent but awkward, unsatisfying, more kindly than passionate. What lives undimmed in Clarissa's mind more than three decades later is a kiss at dusk on a patch of dead grass, and a walk around a pond as mosquitoes droned in the darkening air. There is still that singular perfection, and it's perfect in part because it seemed, at the time, so clearly to promise more. Now she knows: That was the moment, right then. There has been no other.

Mrs. Brown

The cake is less than she'd hoped it would be. She tries not to mind. It is only a cake, she tells herself. It is only a cake. She and Richie have frosted it and she has, guiltily, invented something else for him to do while she squeezes yellow rosebuds onto the edges from a pastry tube and writes "Happy Birthday Dan" in white icing. She does not want the mess her son would make of it. Still, it has not turned out the way she'd pictured it; no, not at all. There's nothing really wrong with it, but she'd imagined something more. She'd imagined it larger, more remarkable. She'd hoped (she admits to herself) it would look more lush and beautiful, more wonderful. This cake she's produced feels small, not just in the physical sense but as an entity. It looks amateurish; handmade. She tells herself, It's fine. It's a fine cake, everyone will love it. Its clumsy aspects (the scattering of crumbs caught in the icing, the squashed appearance of the "n" in "Dan," which got too close to a rose) are part of its charm. She washes the dishes. She thinks about the rest of the day.

She will make the beds, vacuum the rugs. She will wrap the presents she's bought for her husband: a necktie and a new shirt, both more expensive and elegant than the ones he buys for himself; a boar-bristle brush; a small pungent leather case that contains nail clippers, a nail file, and tweezers, for him to take with him when he travels, as he does occasionally, for the agency. He will be happy with all these gifts, or appear to be happy; he will whistle and say "Get a load of this" when he sees the expensive shirt and tie. He will kiss her, enthusiastically, with each present, and tell her she's done too much, she shouldn't have, he doesn't deserve such fine things. Why, she wonders, does it seem that she could give him anything, anything at all, and receive essentially the same response. Why does he desire nothing, really, beyond what he's already got? He is impenetrable in his ambitions and satisfactions, his love of job and home. This, she reminds herself, is a virtue. It is part of his loveliness (she would never use that word in his presence, but privately she thinks of him as lovely, a lovely man, for she has seen him at his most private moments, whimpering over a dream, sitting in the bathtub with his sex shrunk to a stub, floating, heartbreakingly innocent). It is good, she reminds herself—it is lovely—that her husband cannot be touched by ephemera; that his happiness depends only on the fact of her, here in the house, living her life, thinking of him.

Her cake is a failure, but she is loved anyway. She is loved, she thinks, in more or less the way the gifts will be appreciated: because they've been given with good intentions, because they exist, because they are part of a world in which one wants what one gets.

What would she prefer, then? Would she rather have her gifts scorned, her cake sneered at? Of course not. She wants to be loved. She wants to be a competent mother reading calmly to her child; she wants to be a wife who sets a perfect table. She does not want, not at all, to be the strange woman, the pathetic creature, full of quirks and rages, solitary, sulking, tolerated but not loved.

Virginia Woolf put a stone into the pocket of her coat, walked into a river, and drowned.

Laura will not let herself go morbid. She'll make the beds, vacuum, cook the birthday dinner. She will not mind, about anything.

Someone taps at the back door. Laura, washing the last of the dishes, can see the faint outline of Kitty through the filmy white curtain. Here is the vague halo of Kitty's brown-blond hair, the scrubbed pink blur of her face. Laura swallows a pang of excitement and something stronger than excitement, something that resembles panic. She is about to receive a visit from Kitty. Her hair is hardly brushed; she is still wearing her bathrobe. She looks, too much, like the woman of sorrows. She wants to rush to the door and she wants to stand here, immobile, at the sink, until Kitty gives up and goes away. She might actually have done it, stood motionless, holding her breath (can Kitty see inside, would she know?), but there is the problem of Richie, witness to everything, running now into the kitchen, holding a red plastic truck, shouting with a mix of delight and alarm that someone's at the door.

Laura dries her hands on a dish towel covered with red roosters, and opens the door. It's only Kitty, she tells herself. It's only her friend from two doors down, and this, of course, is what people do. They drop by and are received; it doesn't matter about your hair or your robe. It doesn't matter about the cake.

"Hi, Kitty," she says.

"Am I interrupting anything?" Kitty asks.

"Of course not. Come on in."

Kitty enters, and brings with her an aura of cleanliness and a domestic philosophy; a whole vocabulary of avid, nervy movements. She is an attractive, robust, fleshy, large-headed woman several years younger than Laura (it seems that everyone, suddenly, is at least slightly younger than she). Kitty's features, her small eyes and delicate nose, are crowded into the center of her round face. In school she was one of several authoritative, aggressive, not quite beautiful girls so potent in their money and their athletic confidence they simply stood where they stood and insisted that the local notion of desirability be reconfigured to include them. Kitty and her friends—steady, stolid, firm-featured, large-spirited, capable of deep loyalties and terrible cruelties—were the queens of the various festivals, the cheerleaders, the stars of the plays.

"I need a favor," Kitty says.

"Sure," Laura says. "Can you sit a minute?"

"Mm-hm." Kitty sits at the kitchen table. She says a friendly, slightly dismissive hello to the little boy as he watches suspiciously, even angrily (why has she come?) from a place of relative safety near the stove. Kitty, with no children of her own yet (people are starting to wonder), does not attempt to seduce the children of others. They can come to her, if they like; she will not go to them.

"I've got coffee on," Laura says. "Would you like a cup?"

"Sure."

She pours a cup of coffee for Kitty, and one for herself. She glances nervously at the cake, wishing she could hide it. There are crumbs caught in the icing. The "n" in "Dan" is squashed against a rose.

Following Laura's eyes, Kitty says, "Oh, look, you made a cake."

"It's Dan's birthday."

Kitty gets up, comes and stands beside Laura. Kitty wears a white short-sleeved blouse, green plaid shorts, and straw sandals that make a small, crisp sound when she walks.

"Aw, look," she says.

"One of my maiden attempts," Laura says. "It's harder than you'd think, writing in frosting."

She hopes she is careless, debonair, charmingly unconcerned. Why did she put the roses on first, when any idiot would have known to begin with the message? She finds a cigarette. She is someone who smokes and drinks coffee in the mornings, who is raising a family, who has Kitty as a friend, who doesn't mind if her cakes are less than perfect. She lights her cigarette.

"It's cute," Kitty says, and punctures Laura's brash, cigarette self at its inception. The cake is cute, Kitty tells her, the way a child's painting might be cute. It is sweet and touching in its heartfelt, agonizingly sincere discrepancy between ambition and facility. Laura understands: There are two choices only. You can be capable or uncaring. You can produce a masterful cake by your own hand or, barring that, light a cigarette, declare yourself hopeless at such projects, pour yourself another cup of coffee, and order a cake from the bakery. Laura is an artisan who has tried, and failed, publicly. She has produced something cute, when she had hoped (it's embarrassing, but true) to produce something of beauty.

"When is Ray's birthday?" she says, because she has to say something.

"September," Kitty answers. She returns to the kitchen table. What more can be said about the cake?

Laura follows with the coffee cups. Kitty needs friends (her own husband's earnest, slightly stunned charm is not holding up particularly well in the larger world, and there is the matter of their continued childlessness), and so Laura is someone she visits, someone from whom she asks favors. Still, they both know how relentlessly Kitty would have snubbed her in high school, had they been the same age. In another life, not very much unlike this one, they'd have been enemies, but in this life, with its surprises and perversities of timing, Laura is married to a celebrated boy, a war hero, from Kitty's graduating class and has joined the aristocracy in much the way a homely German princess, no longer young, might find herself seated on a throne beside an English king.

What surprises her—what occasionally horrifies her—is how much she revels in Kitty's friendship. Kitty is precious, just as Laura's husband is lovely. Kitty's preciousness, the golden hush of her, the sense of enlarged moment she brings to a room, is like that of a movie star. She has a movie star's singularity, a movie star's flawed and idiosyncratic beauty; like a movie star she seems both common and heightened, in the way of Olivia De Havilland or Barbara Stanwyck. She is deeply, almost profoundly, popular.

"How *is* Ray?" Laura asks as she sets a cup in front of Kitty. "I haven't seen him in a while."

Kitty's husband is Laura's chance to right the balance between them; to offer Kitty her sympathy. Ray is not an embarrassment, exactly—not a complete failure—but he is somehow Kitty's version of Laura's cake, writ large. He was Kitty's high-school boyfriend. He played center on the basketball team, and went on to do well but not spectacularly at USC. He spent seven months as a prisoner of war in the Philippines. He is now some sort of mysterious functionary in the Department of Water and Power, and already, at thirty, is beginning to demonstrate how heroic boys can, by infinitesimal degrees, for no visible reasons, metamorphose into middle-aged drubs. Ray is crew-cut, reliable, myopic; he is full of liquids. He sweats copiously. Small bubbles of clear spit form at the sides of his mouth whenever he speaks at length. Laura imagines (it's impossible not to) that when they make love he must spurt rivers, as opposed to her own husband's modest burble. Why, then, are there still no children?

"He's fine," Kitty says. "He's Ray. He's the same."

"Dan's the same, too," Laura says kindly, empathically. "These guys are something, aren't they?"

She thinks of the gifts she's bought her husband; the gifts he will appreciate, even cherish, but which he does not in any way want. Why did she marry him? She married him out of love. She married him out of guilt; out of fear of being alone; out of patriotism. He was simply too good, too kind, too earnest, too sweet-smelling not to marry. He had suffered so much. He wanted her.

She touches her belly.

Kitty says, "You can say that again."

"Don't you ever wonder what makes them tick? I mean, Dan's like a bulldozer. Nothing seems to bother him."

Kitty shrugs dramatically, rolls her eyes. She and Laura, at this moment, could be high-school girls, best friends, complaining about boys who will soon be replaced by other boys. Laura would like to ask Kitty a question, one she can't quite phrase. The question has to do with subterfuge and, more obscurely, with brilliance. She would like to know if Kitty feels like a strange woman, powerful and unbalanced the way artists are said to be, full of vision, full of rage, committed above all to creating . . . what? This. This kitchen, this birthday cake, this conversation. This revived world.

Laura says, "We've got to get together soon, really. It's been ages."

"This is such good coffee," Kitty says, sipping. "What brand do you use?"

"I don't know. No, of course I know. Folgers. What brand do you use?"

"Maxwell House. It's good, too."

"Mm-hm."

"Still. I'm thinking of switching. I don't know why, really."

"Well. This is Folgers."

"Right. It's good."

Kitty looks into her coffee cup with elaborately false, foolish absorption. She seems, briefly, like a simple, ordinary woman seated at a kitchen table. Her magic evaporates; it is possible to see how she'll look at fifty—she'll be fat, mannish, leathery, wry and ironic about her marriage, one of those women of whom people say, *She used to be quite pretty, you know.* The world is already, subtly, beginning to leave her behind. Laura stabs out her cigarette, thinks of lighting another, decides against it. She makes good coffee carelessly; she takes good care of her husband and child; she lives in this house where no one wants, no one owes, no one suffers. She is pregnant with another child. What does it matter if she is neither glamorous nor a paragon of domestic competence?

"So," she says to Kitty. She is surprised at the power in her own voice; the hint of steel.

"Well," Kitty says.

"What is it? Is everything all right?"

Kitty sits motionless for a moment, looking neither at Laura nor away from her. She gathers into herself. She sits the way one sits among strangers on a train.

She says, "I have to go into the hospital for a couple of days."

"What's the matter?"

"They don't know, exactly. I have some kind of growth."

"My lord."

"It's in, you know. My insides."

"I beg your pardon?"

"My *uterus*. They're going to go in and have a look."

"When?"

"This afternoon. Dr. Rich said sooner's better than later. I need you to feed the dog."

"Of course. What did the doctor *say*, exactly?"

"Just that there's something there, and they need to find out what. It's probably—what the trouble's been. About getting pregnant."

"Well," Laura says. "Then they can get rid of it."

"He says they have to see. He says there's no point in worrying, not at all, but that they have to see."

Laura watches Kitty, who does not move or speak, does not cry.

"It'll be all right," Laura says.

"Yes. Probably it will. I'm not worried. What would be the point of worrying?"

Laura is filled with sorrow and tenderness. Here is Kitty the powerful, Kitty the May Queen, ill and frightened. Here is Kitty's pretty gold wristwatch; here is the quick unraveling of her life. Laura has always imagined, as have most others, that Ray is the problem—Ray with his obscure job in a municipal office; his bubbles of spit; his bow ties; his bourbon. Kitty has seemed, until this moment, like a figure of bright and tragic dignity—a woman standing by her man. So many of these men are not quite what they were (no one likes to talk about it); so many women live uncomplainingly with the quirks and silences, the fits of depression, the drinking. Kitty has seemed, simply, heroic.

The trouble, however, turns out to reside with Kitty, after all. Laura knows, or believes she knows, that there is in fact something to worry about. She sees that Kitty and Ray, their trim little house, are invaded by misfortune; they are half devoured by it. Kitty may not, after all, become that hale, leathery fifty-year-old.

"Come here," Laura says, as she would say to her child, and as if Kitty were Laura's child she does not wait for Kitty to obey but goes to her. She takes Kitty's shoulders in her hands and, after an awkward moment, bends down until she is practically kneeling. She is aware of how big she is, how tall, next to Kitty. She embraces her.

Kitty hesitates, then lets herself be held. She surrenders. She does not cry. Laura can feel the relinquishment; she can feel Kitty give herself over. She thinks, This is how a man feels, holding a woman.

Kitty snakes her arms around Laura's waist. Laura is flooded with feeling. Here, right here in her arms, are Kitty's fear and courage, Kitty's illness. Here are her breasts. Here is the stout, practical heart that beats beneath; here are the watery lights of her being—deep pink lights, red-gold lights, glittering, unsteady; lights that gather and disperse; here are the depths of Kitty, the heart beneath the heart; the untouchable essence that a man (Ray, of all people!) dreams of, yearns toward, searches for so desperately at night. Here it is, in daylight, in Laura's arms. Without quite meaning to, without deciding to, she kisses Kitty, lingeringly, on the top of her forehead. She is full of Kitty's perfume and the crisp, clean essence of Kitty's brown-blond hair.

"I'm fine," Kitty whispers. "Really."

"I know you are," Laura answers.

"If anything, I'm worried about Ray. He doesn't actually manage all that well, not with something like this."

"Forget about Ray for a minute," Laura says. "Just forget about him."

Kitty nods against Laura's breasts. The question has been silently asked and silently answered, it seems. They are both afflicted and blessed, full of shared secrets, striving every moment. They are each impersonating someone. They are weary and beleaguered; they have taken on such enormous work.

Kitty lifts her face, and their lips touch. They both know what they are doing. They rest their mouths, each on the other. They touch their lips together, but do not quite kiss.

It is Kitty who pulls away.

"You're sweet," she says.

Laura releases Kitty. She steps back. She has gone too far, they've both gone too far, but it is Kitty who's pulled away first. It is Kitty whose terrors have briefly propelled her, caused her to act strangely and desperately. Laura is the dark-eyed predator. Laura is the odd one, the foreigner, the one who can't be trusted. Laura and Kitty agree, silently, that this is true.

Laura glances over at Richie. He is still holding the red truck. He is still watching.

"Please don't worry," Laura says to Kitty. "You'll be fine."

Kitty stands, gracefully, without haste. "You know the routine, right? Just give him half a can in the evening, and check his water every now and then. Ray can feed him in the morning."

"Is Ray driving you to the hospital?"

"Mm-hm."

"Don't worry. I'll take care of things here."

"Thank you."

Kitty looks briefly around the room with an expression of weary approval, as if she had decided, somewhat against her better judgment, to buy this house after all, and see what she can do about fixing it up.

"Bye," she says.

"I'll call you tomorrow, at the hospital."

"Okay."

With a reluctant smile, a small compression of her lips, Kitty turns and leaves.

Laura faces her little boy, who stares at her nervously, suspiciously, adoringly. She is, above all else, tired; she wants more than anything to return to her bed and her book. The world, this world, feels suddenly stunned and stunted, far from everything. There is the heat falling evenly on the streets and houses; there is the single string of stores referred to, locally, as downtown. There is the supermarket and the drugstore and the dry cleaner's; there is the beauty parlor and the stationery shop and the five-and-dime; there is the one-story stucco library, with its newspapers on wooden poles and its shelves of slumbering books.

. . . life, London, this moment of June.

Laura leads her son back into the living room, reintroduces him to his tower of colored wooden blocks. Once he is settled, she returns to the kitchen and, without hesitation, picks up the cake and tips it from its milk-glass platter into the garbage can. It lands with a surprisingly solid sound; a yellow rose is smeared along the can's curved side. She immediately feels relieved, as if steel cords have been loosened from around her chest. She can start over now. According to the clock on the wall, it is barely ten-thirty. She has plenty of time to make another cake. This time, she will prevent crumbs from getting caught in the icing. This time, she will trace the letters with a toothpick, so they'll be centered, and she'll leave the roses for last.

Mrs. Woolf

She is reading proofs with Leonard and Ralph when Lottie announces that Mrs. Bell and the children have arrived.

"That can't be," Virginia says. "It's not two-thirty yet. They're coming at four."

"They're here, ma'am," says Lottie in her slightly numbed tone. "Mrs. Bell has gone straight into the parlor."

Marjorie glances up from the parcel of books she's been wrapping in twine (she, unlike Ralph, will compliantly wrap parcels and sort type, which is a blessing and a disappointment). She says, "Is it two-thirty already? I'd hoped to have these off by now." Virginia does not wince, not visibly, at the sound of Marjorie's voice.

Leonard says sternly to Virginia, "I can't stop working. I will make my contracted appearance at four o'clock, and if Vanessa chooses to remain that long, I'll see her then."

"Don't worry, I'll attend to Vanessa," Virginia says, and as she stands she's aware of her disheveled housedress, the lank disorder of her hair. It's only my sister, she thinks, but still, after all this time, after everything that's happened, she wants to inspire in Vanessa a certain surprised admiration. Still she wants her sister to think, "The goat's really looking rather well, isn't she?"

Virginia is not looking particularly well, and there's not much she can do about it, but at least by four o'clock she'd have fixed her hair and changed her dress. She follows Lottie upstairs, and as she passes the oval mirror that hangs in the foyer she is tempted, briefly, to look at her reflection. But she can't. Squaring her shoulders, she enters the parlor. Vanessa will be her mirror, just as she's always been. Vanessa is her ship, her strip of green coastline where bees hum among the grapes.

She kisses Vanessa, chastely, on the mouth.

"Darling," says Virginia, holding her sister's shoulders in her hands. "If I tell you I'm enchanted to see you now, I'm sure you can imagine how ecstatic I'd have been to see you at the hour you were actually expected."

Vanessa laughs. Vanessa is firm of face, her skin a brilliant, scalded pink. Although she is three years older, she looks younger than Virginia, and both of them know it. If Virginia has the austere, parched beauty of a Giotto fresco, Vanessa is more like a figure sculpted in rosy marble by a skilled but minor artist of the late Baroque. She is a distinctly earthly and even decorative figure, all billows and scrolls, her face and body rendered in an affectionate, slightly sentimentalized attempt to depict a state of human abundance so lavish it edges over into the ethereal.

"Forgive me," Vanessa says. "We got finished in London earlier than I'd ever imagined we would, and our only other choice was to drive in circles around Richmond until four o'clock."

"And what have you done with the children?" Virginia asks.

"They've gone around to the garden. Quentin found a dying bird in the road, and they seem to believe it needs to be in the garden."

"I'm sure their old Aunt Virginia is no competition for that. Shall we go out to them?"

As they leave the house, Vanessa takes Virginia's hand in much the way she would take the hand of one of her children. It is almost as irritating as it is satisfying that Vanessa feels so proprietary; so certain she can arrive a full hour and a half before she's invited. Here she is, then; here is her hand. If only Virginia had had time to do a little something with her hair.

She says, "I've packed Nelly off to London for sugared ginger for our tea. You can expect it in about an hour, along with a nice little draught of Nelly's heart's blood."

"Nelly must bear it," Vanessa says. Yes, Virginia thinks, that's it, just that tone of stern, rueful charity—that is how one speaks to servants, and to sisters. There's an art to it, as there's an art to everything, and much of what Vanessa has to teach is contained in these seemingly effortless gestures. One arrives early or late, claiming airily that it could not be helped. One offers one's hand with motherly assurance. One says, Nelly must bear it, and by so doing forgives servant and mistress alike.

In the garden, Vanessa's children kneel in a circle on the grass near the rosebushes. How astonishing they are: three beings, fully clothed, conjured out of nothing. One moment there are two young sisters cleaving to each other, breast against breast, lips ready, and then the next moment, it seems, there are two middle-aged married women standing together on a modest bit of lawn before a body of children (Vanessa's, of course, all Vanessa's; there are none of Virginia's, and there will be none). Here is grave, handsome Julian; here is ruddy Quentin holding the bird (a thrush) in his red hands; here is little Angelica, crouched slightly apart from her brothers, frightened, fascinated by this handful of gray feathers. Years ago, when Julian was a baby, when Virginia and Vanessa were thinking of names for children and for characters in novels, Virginia had suggested that Vanessa name her future daughter Clarissa.

"Hello, changelings," Virginia calls.

"We've found a bird," Angelica announces. "It's ill."

"So I understand," Virginia answers.

"It's alive," Quentin says with scholarly gravity. "I think we might be able to save it."

Vanessa squeezes Virginia's hand. Oh, thinks Virginia, just before tea, here's death. What, exactly, does one say to children, or to anybody?

"We can make it comfortable," Vanessa says. "But this is the bird's time to die, we can't change that."

Just so, the seamstress cuts the thread. This much, children, no less but no more. Vanessa does not harm her children but she does not lie to them either, not even for mercy's sake.

"We should fix a box for it," Quentin says, "and bring it into the house."

"I don't think so," Vanessa answers. "It's a wild thing, it will want to die outdoors."

"We shall have a funeral," says Angelica brightly. "I shall sing."

"It's still alive," Quentin tells her sharply.

Bless you, Quentin, thinks Virginia. Will it be you who one day holds my hand and attends to my actual final breathing while everyone else secretly rehearses the speeches they'll deliver at the service?

Julian says, "We should make a bed of grass for it. Angie, will you pick some?"

"Yes, Julian," Angelica says. She obediently sets about pulling up handfuls of grass.

Julian; ah, Julian. Was there ever more persuasive evidence of nature's fundamental inequity than Julian, Vanessa's oldest, at age fifteen? Julian is bluff and sturdy, royal; he possesses a gracefully muscular, equine beauty so natural it suggests that beauty itself is a fundamental human condition and not a mutation in the general design. Quentin (bless him), for all his intellect and irony, could already, at thirteen, be a stout, red-faced colonel in the Royal Cavalry, and Angelica, perfectly formed, evinces even at five a nervously wrought, milky prettiness that almost certainly will not last beyond her youth. Julian, the firstborn, is so clearly and effortlessly the hero of this family's story, the repository of its grandest hopes—who can blame Vanessa for favoring him?

"Shall we pick some roses, too?" Virginia says to Angelica.

"Yes," Angelica answers, still busy with the grass. "The yellow ones."

Before going with Angelica into the rose garden, Virginia stands another moment, still holding hands with Vanessa, watching Vanessa's children as if they were a pool of water into which she might or might not dive. This, Virginia thinks, is the true accomplishment; this will live after the tinselly experiments in narrative have been packed off along with the old photographs and fancy dresses, the china plates on which Grandmother painted her wistful, invented landscapes.

She disengages her hand and goes into the garden, where she kneels beside Angelica and helps her create a bed in which the thrush can die. Quentin and Julian stand close by, but Angelica is clearly the most enthusiastic member of the funeral party, the one whose tastes in decoration and decorum must be respected. Angelica is, somehow, the widow here.

"There, now," Virginia says, as she and Angelica arrange grass into a billowy little mound. "She should be quite comfortable, I think."

"Is it a she?" Angelica asks.

"Yes. The females are larger and a bit more drab."

"Does she have eggs?"

Virginia hesitates. "I don't know," she says. "We can't tell, really, can we?"

"When she's died, I shall look for her eggs."

"If you like. There may be a nest in the eaves somewhere."

"I shall find them," Angelica says, "and hatch them."

Quentin laughs. "Will you sit on them yourself?" he says.

"No, stupid. I shall hatch them."

"Ah," says Quentin, and without seeing them Virginia knows he and Julian are laughing, quietly, at Angelica and perhaps, by extension, at her. Even now, in this late age, the males still hold death in their capable hands and laugh affectionately at the females, who arrange funerary beds and who speak of resuscitating the specks of nascent life abandoned in the landscape, by magic or sheer force of will.

"All right, then," Virginia says. "We're ready for the laying-out."

"No," says Angelica. "There's still the roses."

"Right," Virginia answers. She almost protests that the bird should be laid down first, the roses arranged around its body. That is clearly how it should be done. You would, she thinks, argue with a five-year-old girl about such things. You would, if Vanessa and the boys weren't watching.

Angelica takes one of the yellow roses they've picked and places it, carefully, along the edge of the grass mound. She adds another and another until she has created a rough circle of rosebuds, thorny stems, and leaves.

"That's nice," she says, and surprisingly, it is. Virginia looks with unanticipated pleasure at this modest circlet of thorns and flowers; this wild deathbed. She would like to lie down on it herself.

"Shall we put her in, then?" she says softly to Angelica.

Virginia leans toward Angelica as if they shared a secret. Some force flows between them, a complicity that is neither maternal nor erotic but contains elements of both. There is an understanding here. There is some sort of understanding too large for language. Virginia can feel it, as surely as she feels weather on her skin, but when she looks deeply into Angelica's face she sees by Angelica's bright, unfocused eyes that she is already growing impatient with the game. She's made her arrangement of grass and roses; now she wants to dispatch the bird as quickly as possible and go hunting for its nest.

"Yes," Angelica says. Already, at five, she can feign grave enthusiasm for the task at hand, when all she truly wants is for everyone to admire her work and then set her free. Quentin kneels with the bird and gently, immeasurably gently, lays it on the grass. Oh, if men were the brutes and women the angels—if it were as simple as that. Virginia thinks of Leonard frowning over the proofs, intent on scouring away not only the setting errors but whatever taint of mediocrity errors imply. She thinks of Julian last summer, rowing across the Ouse, his sleeves rolled up to his elbows, and how it had seemed to be the day, the moment, he became a man and not a child.

When Quentin takes his hands away, Virginia can see that the bird is laid on the grass compactly, its wings folded up against its body. She knows it has died already, in Quentin's palms. It seems to have wanted to make the smallest possible package of itself. Its eye, a perfect black bead, is open, and its gray feet, larger than you'd expect them to be, are curled in on themselves.

Vanessa comes up behind Virginia. "Let's leave her now, everyone," Vanessa says. "We've done what we can."

Angelica and Quentin disperse willingly. Angelica starts her circuit of the house, squinting up at the eaves. Quentin wipes his hands on his jersey and goes inside to wash up. (Does he believe the bird has left a residue of death on his hands? Does he believe good English soap and one of Aunt Virginia's towels will wash it away?) Julian stays with Vanessa and Virginia, still in attendance on the little corpse.

He says, "Angie got so excited about the nest she forgot to sing her hymn."

Vanessa says, "Should we be denied any tea at all, for coming so early?"

"No," Virginia answers. "I'm fully equipped to make tea without assistance from Nelly."

"Well, then," Vanessa says, and she and Julian turn and walk back to the house, Julian's hand slipped into the crook of his mother's elbow. Before following them, Virginia lingers another moment beside the dead bird in its circle of roses. It could be a kind of hat. It could be the missing link between millinery and death.

She would like to lie down in its place. No denying it, she would like that. Vanessa and Julian can go on about their business, their tea and travels, while she, Virginia, a bird-sized Virginia, lets herself metamorphose from an angular, difficult woman into an ornament on a hat; a foolish, uncaring thing.

Clarissa, she thinks, is not the bride of death after all. Clarissa is the bed in which the bride is laid.

Mrs. Dalloway

Clarissa fills a vase with a dozen of the yellow roses. She takes it into the living room, puts it on the coffee table, steps back, and tries it several inches to the left. She will give Richard the best party she can manage. She will try to create something temporal, even trivial, but perfect in its way. She will see to it that he is surrounded by people who genuinely respect and admire him (why did she ask Walter Hardy, how could she be so weak?); she will make sure he doesn't get overtired. It is her tribute, her gift. What more can she offer him?

She is on her way back to the kitchen when the intercom buzzes. Who would this be? A delivery she's forgotten about, probably, or the caterer dropping something off. She presses the button for the speaker.

"Who is it?" she says.

"Louis. It's Louis."

"Louis? Really?"

Clarissa buzzes him in. Of course it's Louis. No one else, certainly no New Yorker, would just ring the bell without calling first. No one does that. She opens the door and goes out into the hall with a great and almost dizzying sense of anticipation, a feeling so strong and so peculiar, so unknown under any other circumstances, that she decided some time ago to simply name it after Louis. It's that Louis feeling, and through it run traces of devotion and guilt, attraction, a distinct element of stage fright, and a pure untarnished hope, as if every time Louis appears he might, finally, be bringing a piece of news so good it's impossible to anticipate its extent or even its precise nature.

Then, a moment later, coming around the bend in the hallway, is Louis himself. It has been, what, over five years now, but he's exactly the same. Same electric bristle of white hair, same avid and quirky walk, same careless clothes that somehow look right. His old beauty, his heft and leonine poise, vanished with such surprising suddenness almost two decades ago, and this Louis—white-haired, sinewy, full of furtive, chastened emotions—emerged in much the way a small, unimposing man might jump from the turret of a tank to announce that it was he, not the machine, who flattened your village. Louis, the old object of desire, has always, as it turns out, been this: a drama teacher, a harmless person.

"Well, now," he says.

He and Clarissa embrace. When Clarissa pulls back she sees that Louis's myopic gray eyes are moist. He has always been prone to tears. Clarissa, the more sentimental one, the more indignant, never seems to cry at all, though she often wants to.

"When did you get into town?" she asks.

"Day before yesterday. I was out walking, and I realized I was on your street."

"I'm so happy to see you."

"I'm happy to see you, too," Louis says, and his eyes fill again.

"Your timing is incredible. We're having a party for Richard tonight."

"Really? What's the occasion?"

"He won the Carrouthers. Didn't you hear?"

"The what?"

"It's a prize for poets. It's a very big deal. I'm surprised you haven't heard of it."

"Well. Congratulations Richard."

"I hope you'll come. He'd be thrilled to see you."

"Would he?"

"Yes. Of course. Why are we standing here, practically in the hallway? Come in."

She looks older, Louis thinks as he follows Clarissa into the apartment (eight steps, turn, then another three steps). She looks older, Louis thinks in astonishment. It's finally happening. What a remarkable thing, these genetic trip wires, the way a body can sail along essentially unaltered, decade after decade, and then in a few years capitulate to age. Louis is surprised at how sad he feels, how little satisfied, by the relatively abrupt departure of Clarissa's unnaturally prolonged prime. How many times has he fantasized about it? It's his revenge, the only possible settling of the score. All those years with Richard, all that love and effort, and Richard spends the last years of his life writing about a woman with a town house on West Tenth Street. Richard produces a novel that meditates exhaustively on a woman (a fifty-plus-page chapter on shopping for nail polish, which she decides against!) and old Louis W. is relegated to the chorus. Louis W. has one scene, a relatively short one, in which he whines about the paucity of love in the world. That's what there is; that's the reward, after more than a dozen years; after living with Richard in six different apartments, holding him, fucking him senseless; after thousands of meals together; after the trip to Italy and that hour under the tree. After all that, Louis appears, and will be remembered, as a sad man complaining about love.

"Where are you staying?" Clarissa asks.

"With James, at the roach motel."

"He's still there?"

"Some of his *groceries* are still there. I saw a box of farfalle I remember picking up at the store for him five years ago. He tried to deny that it was the same box, but it has a dent in one corner I remember perfectly."

Louis touches his nose with a fingertip (left side, right side). Clarissa turns to face him. "Look at you," Clarissa says, and they embrace again. They hold each other for almost a full minute (his lips brush her left shoulder, and he shifts to brush his lips against her right shoulder, too). It is Clarissa who disengages.

"Do you want something to drink?" she asks.

"No. Yes. A glass of water?"

Clarissa goes into the kitchen. How impenetrable she still is, how infuriatingly well behaved. Clarissa has been right here, Louis thinks, all this time. She's been here in these rooms with her girlfriend (or partner, or whatever they call themselves), going to work and coming home again. She's been having a day and then another, going to plays, going to parties.

There is, he thinks, so little love in the world.

Louis takes four steps into the living room. Here he is again, in the big cool room with the garden, the deep sofa, and good rugs. He blames Sally for the apartment. It's Sally's influence, Sally's taste. Sally and Clarissa live in a perfect replica of an upper-class West Village apartment; you imagine somebody's assistant striding through with a clipboard: French leather armchairs, check; Stickley table, check; linen-colored walls hung with botanical prints, check; bookshelves studded with small treasures acquired abroad, check. Even the eccentricities—the flea-market mirror frame covered in seashells, the scaly old South American chest painted with leering mermaids—feel calculated, as if the art director had looked it all over and said, "It isn't convincing enough yet, we need more things to tell us who these people really *are*."

Clarissa returns with two glasses of water (carbonated, with ice and lemon), and at the sight of her Louis smells the air—pine and grass, slightly brackish water—of Wellfleet more than thirty years ago. His heart rises. She is older but—no point in denying it—she still has that rigorous glamour; that slightly butch, aristocratic sexiness. She is still slim. She still exudes, somehow, an aspect of thwarted romance, and looking at her now, past fifty, in this dim and prosperous room, Louis thinks of photographs of young soldiers, firm-featured boys serene in their uniforms; boys who died before the age of twenty and who live on as the embodiment of wasted promise, in photo albums or on side tables, beautiful and confident, unfazed by their doom, as the living survive jobs and errands, disappointing holidays. At this moment Clarissa reminds Louis of a soldier. She seems to look out at the aging world from a past realm; she seems as sad and innocent and invincible as the dead do in photographs.

She gives Louis a glass of water. "You look good," she says. Louis's middle-aged face has always been incipient in his younger face: the beaky nose and pale, astonished eyes; the wiry brows; the neck powerfully veined under a broad, bony chin. He was meant to be a farmer, strong as a weed, ravaged by weather, and age has done in fifty years what plowing and harvesting would have in half the time.

"Thanks," Louis says.

"It feels as if you've been so far away."

"I have been. It's good to be back."

"Five years," Clarissa says. "I can't believe you didn't visit New York even once."

Louis takes three swallows of water. He's come back to New York several times over the past five years, but did not call. Although he'd never resolved specifically not to see Clarissa or Richard he did in fact fail to call. It seemed simpler that way.

"I'm coming back for good," Louis says. "I'm fed up with these teaching gigs, I'm too old and too mean. I'm too *poor*. I'm thinking of getting some kind of honest job."

"Really?"

"Oh, I don't know. Don't worry, I'm not going back to school for my MBA, or anything."

"I thought you'd fall in love with San Francisco. I thought we'd never see you again."

"Everybody expects you to fall in love with San Francisco. It's depressing."

"Louis, Richard is very different than he was."

"Is it pretty awful?"

"I just want you to be prepared."

"You've stayed close to him, all these years," Louis says.

"Yes. I have."

She is, Louis decides, a handsome, ordinary woman. She is exactly that, neither more nor less. Clarissa sits down on the sofa and, after a moment's hesitation, Louis takes five steps and sits beside her.

"Of course, I've read the book," he says.

"Have you? Good."

"Isn't it weird?"

"Yes. It is."

"He hardly even bothered to change your name."

"That isn't me," she says. "It's Richard's fantasy about some woman who vaguely resembles me."

"It's a damned weird *book*."

"So everybody seems to think."

"It feels like it's about ten thousand pages long. Nothing happens. And then, *bam*. She kills herself."

"His mother."

"I *know*. Still. It's completely out of the blue."

"You're in perfect agreement with almost every critic. They'd waited all that time, and for what? More than nine hundred pages of flirtation, really, with a sudden death at the end. People did say it was beautifully written."

Louis looks away from her. "These roses are beautiful," he says.

Clarissa leans forward and moves the vase slightly to the left. Good lord, Louis thinks, she's gone beyond wifeliness. She's become her mother.

Clarissa laughs. "Look at me," she says. "An old woman fussing with her roses."

She always surprises you this way, by knowing more than you think she does. Louis wonders if they're calculated, these little demonstrations of self-knowledge that pepper Clarissa's wise, hostessy performance. She seems, at times, to have read your thoughts. She disarms you by saying, essentially, I know what you're thinking and I agree, I'm ridiculous, I'm far less than I could have been and I'd like it to be otherwise but I can't seem to help myself. You find that you move, almost against your will, from being irritated with her to consoling her, helping her back into her performance so that she can be comfortable again and you can resume feeling irritated.

"So," Louis says. "Richard is pretty sick."

"Yes. His body's not in such terrible shape anymore, but his mind wanders. I'm afraid he was a little too far gone for the protease inhibitors to help him the way they're helping some people."

"It must be terrible."

"He's still himself. I mean, there's this sort of constant quality, some sort of Richardness, that's not the least bit different."

"That's good. That's something."

"Remember the big dune in Wellfleet?" she says.

"Sure."

"I was thinking the other day that when I die I'll probably want my ashes scattered there."

"That's awfully morbid," Louis says.

"But you think about these things. How could you not?"

Clarissa believed then and she believes today that the dune in Wellfleet will, in some sense, accompany her forever. Whatever else happens, she will always have had that. She will always have been standing on a high dune in the summer. She will always have been young and indestructibly healthy, a little hungover, wearing Richard's cotton sweater as he wraps a hand familiarly around her neck and Louis stands slightly apart, watching the waves.

"I was furious at you then," Louis says. "Sometimes I could hardly look at you."

"I know."

"I tried to be good. I tried to be open and free."

"We all tried. I'm not sure the organism is fully capable."

Louis says, "I drove up there once. To the house. I don't think I told you."

"No. You didn't."

"It was right before I left for California. I was on a panel in Boston, some awful thing about the future of theater, just a crew of pompous old dinosaurs they'd trucked in to give the graduate students something to jeer at, and afterward I was so blue I rented a car and drove out to Wellfleet. I hardly had any trouble finding it."

"I probably don't want to know."

"No, it's still there, and it looks pretty much the same. It's been gussied up a little. New paint, you know, and somebody put in a lawn, which looks weird out in the woods, like wall-to-wall carpet. But it's still standing."

"What do you know," Clarissa says.

They sit quietly for a moment. It is somehow worse that the house still stands. It is worse that sun and then dark and sun again have entered and left those rooms every day, that rain has continued falling on that roof, that the whole thing could be visited again.

Clarissa says, "I should go up there sometime. I'd like to stand on the dune."

"If that's where you think you want your ashes scattered, yes, you should go back and confirm."

"No, you were right, I was being morbid. Summer brings it out in me. I have no idea where I'd want my ashes scattered."

Clarissa wants, suddenly, to show her whole life to Louis. She wants to tumble it out onto the floor at Louis's feet, all the vivid, pointless moments that can't be told as stories. She wants to sit with Louis and sift through it.

"So," she says. "Tell me some more about San Francisco."

"It's a pretty little city with great restaurants and nothing going on. My students are mostly imbeciles. Really, I'm coming back to New York as soon as I can."

"Good. It'd be good to have you back here."

Clarissa touches Louis's shoulder, and it seems that they will both rise, without speaking, go upstairs to the bedroom, and undress together. It seems they will go to the bedroom and undress not like lovers but like gladiators who've survived the arena, who find themselves bloody and harmed but miraculously alive when all the others have died. They will wince as they unstrap their breastplates and shin guards. They will look at each other with tenderness and reverence; they will gently embrace as New York clatters outside the casement window; as Richard sits in his chair listening to voices and Sally has her lunch uptown with Oliver St. Ives.

Louis puts his glass down, lifts it, sets it down again. He taps his foot on the carpet, three times.

"It's a little complicated, though," he says. "You see, I've fallen in love."

"Really?"

"His name is Hunter. Hunter Craydon."

"Hunter Craydon. Well."

"He was a student of mine last year," Louis says.

Clarissa leans back, sighs impatiently. This would be the fourth, at least of the ones she knows about. She would like to grab Louis and say, You have to age better than this. I can't stand to see you make so much of yourself and then offer it all to some boy just because he happens to be pretty and young.

"He may be the most gifted student I've ever taught," Louis

says. "He does the most remarkable performance pieces about growing up white and gay in South Africa. Incredibly powerful."

"Well," Clarissa says. She can think of nothing else to say. She feels sorry for Louis, and deeply impatient, and yet, she thinks, Louis is in love. He is in love with a young man. He is fifty-three and still has all that ahead of him, the sex and the ridiculous arguments, the anguish.

"He's amazing," Louis says. To his complete surprise, he begins to weep. The tears start simply enough, as a heat at the back of his eyes and a furring of his vision. These spasms of emotion take him constantly. A song can do it; even the sight of an old dog. They pass. They usually pass. This time, though, tears start falling from his eyes almost before he knows it will happen, and for a moment a compartment of his being (the same compartment that counts steps, sips, claps) says to itself, He's crying, how strange. Louis leans forward, puts his face in his hands. He sobs.

The truth is that he does not love Hunter and Hunter does not love him. They are having an affair; only an affair. He fails to think of him for hours at a time. Hunter has other boyfriends, a whole future planned, and when he's moved on, Louis has to admit, privately, that he won't much miss Hunter's shrill laugh, his chipped front tooth, his petulant silences.

There is so little love in the world.

Clarissa rubs Louis's back with the flat of her hand. What had Sally said? We never fight. It was at dinner somewhere, a year ago or longer. There had been some kind of fish, thick medallions in a puddle of bright yellow sauce (it seemed everything, just then, sat in a puddle of brightly colored sauce). We never fight. It's true. They bicker, they sulk, but they never explode, never shout or weep, never break a dish. It has always seemed that they haven't fought *yet*; that they're still too new for all-out war; that whole unexplored continents lie ahead once they've worked their way through their initial negotiations and feel sufficiently certain in each other's company to really let loose. What could she have been thinking? She and Sally will soon celebrate their eighteenth anniversary together. They are a couple that never fight.

As she rubs Louis's back, Clarissa thinks, Take me with you. I want a doomed love. I want streets at night, wind and rain, no one wondering where I am.

"I'm sorry," Louis says.

"It's all right. For god's sake, look at all that's happened."

"I feel like such an asshole." He stands and walks to the French doors (seven steps). Through his tears he can see the moss in the low stone troughs, the bronze platter of clear water on which floats a single white feather. He can't tell why he's crying. He's back in New York. He seems to be crying over this odd garden, Richard's illness (why was Louis spared?), this room with Clarissa in it, everything. He seems to be crying over a Hunter who only resembles the actual one. This other Hunter has a fierce and tragic grandeur, true intelligence, a modest turn of mind. Louis weeps for him.

Clarissa follows. "It's all right," she says again.

"Stupid," Louis murmurs. "Stupid."

A key turns in the front door. "It's Julia," Clarissa says.

"Shit."

"Don't worry. She's seen men cry."

It's her goddamn daughter. Louis straightens his shoulders, steps sideways from under Clarissa's arm. He continues looking out at the garden, trying to bring his face under control. He thinks about moss. He thinks about fountains. He is suddenly, genuinely interested in moss and fountains.

How strange, the voice says. Why is he thinking about things like that?

"Hello," says Julia, behind him. Not "hi." She has always been a grave little girl, smart but peculiar, oversized, full of quirks and tics.

"Hi, honey," Clarissa says. "Do you remember Louis?"

Louis turns to face her. Fine, let her see that he's been crying. Fuck it.

"Of course I do," Julia says. She walks toward him, extending her hand.

She is eighteen now, maybe nineteen. She is so unexpectedly handsome, so altered, that Louis worries the tears will start all over again. When he saw her last she was thirteen or so, slouchy and overweight, embarrassed by herself. She still isn't beautiful, she'll never be beautiful, but she's acquired a measure of her mother's presence, that golden certainty. She is handsome and assured in the way of a young athlete, her head all but shaved, her skin pink.

"Julia," he says. "How nice to see you."

She takes his hand firmly in hers. She wears a thin silver ring in her nose. She is lush and strong, crackling with health, like some kind of idealized Irish farm girl just in from the fields. She must take after her father (Louis has fantasized about him, imagined him as a strapping young blond, hard up, an actor or painter maybe, a lover, a criminal, a desperate boy, down to selling his fluids, blood to the blood bank and sperm to the sperm bank). He must, Louis thinks, have been huge, rugged, a figure of Celtic myth, for here now is Julia, who even in her tank top and shorts, her black combat boots, looks as if she should be carrying a sheaf of barley under one arm and a new lamb under the other.

"Hello, Louis," she says. She holds his hand but does not shake it. Of course, she knows he's been crying. She does not seem particularly surprised. What must she have heard about him?

"I've got to go," he says.

She nods. "How long are you here?" she asks.

"Just a few days. But I'm moving back. It's good to see you. Bye, Clarissa."

"Five o'clock," Clarissa says.

"What?"

"The party. It's at five. Please come."

"Of course I'll come."

Julia says, "Goodbye, Louis."

She is a handsome nineteen-year-old who says hello and goodbye, not "hi" and "bye." She has unusually small, very white teeth.

"Goodbye."

"You will come, won't you?" Clarissa says. "Promise me you'll come."

"I promise. Goodbye." He gets himself out of the apartment, still vaguely teary; furious with Clarissa; vaguely, absurdly in love with Julia (he who has never been attracted to women, never—he still shudders, after all these years, at the recollection of that awful, desperate attempt he made with Clarissa, simply to retain his claim on Richard). He imagines running, with Julia, out of that dreadful, tasteful apartment; getting himself and her away from the linen-colored walls and the botanical prints, from Clarissa and her glasses of carbonated water with lemon slices. He walks down the dim hallway (twenty-three steps), through the door to the vestibule and then through the outer door, onto West Tenth Street. The sun explodes like a flashbulb in his face. He rejoins, gratefully, the people of the world: a ferrety-looking man walking two dachshunds, a fat man sweating majestically in a dark blue suit, a bald woman (fashion or chemotherapy?) who leans against Clarissa's building sucking on a cigarette and whose face looks like a fresh bruise. Louis will return here, to this city; he will live in an apartment in the West Village, sit in Dante with an espresso and a cigarette in the afternoons. He isn't old, not yet. The night before last he stopped his car in the Arizona desert and stood under the stars until he could feel the presence of his own soul, or whatever you wanted to call it; the continuing part that had been a child and then stood—it seemed a moment later—in the desert silence under the constellations. He thinks with distracted affection of himself, the young Louis Waters, who spent his youth trying to live with Richard, who was variously flattered and enraged by Richard's indefatigable worship of his arms and his ass, and who left Richard finally, forever, after a fight in the train station in Rome (had it been specifically about the letter Richard received from Clarissa, or about Louis's more general sense of exhausted interest in being the more blessed, less brilliant member?). That Louis, only twenty-eight but convinced of his advanced age and missed opportunities, had walked away from Richard and gotten on a train that turned out to be going to Madrid. It had seemed, at the time, a dramatic but temporary gesture, and as the train steamed along (the conductor had informed him, indignantly, where he was headed) he'd been strangely, almost preternaturally content. He'd been free. Now he scarcely remembers his aimless days in Madrid; he does not even remember with great clarity the Italian boy (could his name actually have been Franco?) who convinced him to finally abandon the long, doomed project of loving Richard, in favor of simpler passions. What he remembers with perfect clarity is sitting on a train headed for Madrid, feeling the sort of happiness he imagined spirits might feel, freed of their earthly bodies but still possessed of their essential selves. He walks east toward University (seventy-seven steps to the corner). He waits to cross.

Mrs. Brown

As she pilots her Chevrolet along the Pasadena Freeway, among hills still scorched in places from last year's fire, she feels as if she's dreaming or, more precisely, as if she's remembering this drive from a dream long ago. Everything she sees feels as if it's pinned to the day the way etherized butterflies are pinned to a board. Here are the black slopes of the hills dotted with the pastel stucco houses that were spared from the flames. Here is the hazy, blue-white sky. Laura drives competently, neither too slow nor too fast, periodically checking the rearview mirror. She is a woman in a car dreaming about being in a car.

She has left her son with Mrs. Latch down the street. She has claimed a last-minute errand related to her husband's birthday.

She panicked—she supposes "panic" is the word for it. She tried to lie down for a few minutes while her son was napping; she tried to read a little, but couldn't concentrate. She lay on the bed with the book in her hands feeling emptied, exhausted, by the child, the cake, the kiss. It got down, somehow, to those three elements, and as she lay on the double bed with the shades drawn and the bedside lamp lit, trying to read, she wondered, Is this what it's like to go crazy? She'd never imagined it like this—when she'd thought of someone (a woman like herself) losing her mind, she'd imagined shrieks and wails, hallucinations; but at that moment it had seemed clear that there was another way, far quieter; a way that was numb and hopeless, flat, so much so that an emotion as strong as sorrow would have been a relief.

And so she's left for a few hours. She has not acted irresponsibly. She's made sure her son is taken care of. She's baked a new cake, thawed the steaks, topped the beans. Having done all that, she's permitting herself to leave. She will be home in time to cook the dinner, to feed Kitty's dog. But now, right now, she is going somewhere (where?) to be alone, to be free of her child, her house, the small party she will give tonight. She has taken her pocketbook, and her copy of *Mrs. Dalloway*. She has put on hose and a blouse and skirt; she has clipped her favorite earrings, simple copper disks, onto her ears. She feels faintly, foolishly satisfied by her outfit, and by the cleanliness of her car. A small dark-blue wastebasket, empty of trash, hugs the axle housing the way a saddle fits a horse. It's ridiculous, she knows, and yet she finds consolation in this impeccable order. She is clean and well dressed, driving away.

At home, the new cake waits under an aluminum cake-saver with a wooden knob shaped like an acorn. It is an improvement over the first cake. This cake has been frosted twice, so there are no crumbs caught in the icing (she has consulted a second cookbook, and learned that bakers refer to the first layer of icing as the "crumb layer," and that a cake should always be iced a second time). This cake says "Happy Birthday Dan" in elegant white script, uncrowded by the clusters of yellow roses. It's a fine cake, perfect in its way, and yet Laura is still disappointed in it. It still feels amateurish, homemade; it still seems somehow wrong. The "y" in "Happy" isn't what she'd hoped it would be, and two of the roses are lopsided.

She touches her lips, where Kitty's kiss briefly resided. She doesn't mind so much about the kiss, what it does and does not imply, except that it gives Kitty an edge. Love is deep, a mystery—who wants to understand its every particular? Laura desires Kitty. She desires her force, her brisk and cheerful disappointment, the shifting pink-gold lights of her secret self and the crisp, shampooed depths of her hair. Laura desires Dan, too, in a darker and less exquisite way; a way that is more subtly haunted by cruelty and shame. Still it is desire, sharp as a bone chip. She can kiss Kitty in the kitchen and love her husband, too. She can anticipate the queasy pleasure of her husband's lips and fingers (is it that she desires his desire?) and still dream of kissing Kitty again someday, in a kitchen or at the beach as children shriek in the surf, in a hallway with their arms full of folded towels, laughing softly, aroused, hopeless, in love with their own recklessness if not each other, saying *Shhhh*, parting quickly, going on.

What Laura regrets, what she can hardly bear, is the cake. It embarrasses her, but she can't deny it. It's only sugar, flour, and eggs—part of a cake's charm is its inevitable imperfections. She knows that; of course she does. Still she had hoped to create something finer, something more significant, than what she's produced, even with its smooth surface and its centered message. She wants (she admits to herself) a dream of a cake manifested as an actual cake; a cake invested with an undeniable and profound sense of comfort, of bounty. She wants to have baked a cake that banishes sorrow, even if only for a little while. She wants to have produced something marvelous; something that would be marvelous even to those who do not love her.

She has failed. She wishes she didn't mind. Something, she thinks, is wrong with her.

She shifts over to the left-hand lane, presses the accelerator. For now, right now, she could be anyone, going anywhere. She has a full tank of gas, money in her wallet. For an hour or two, she can go wherever she likes. After that, the alarms will start up. By five o'clock or so, Mrs. Latch will begin to worry, and by six at the latest she'll start making calls. If it gets that late Laura will have explaining to do, but right now and for at least another two hours, really, she is free. She's a woman in a car, only that.

When she tops the rise at Chavez Ravine, and the hazy spires of downtown appear, she has to make a choice. For the past half hour it has been enough to be headed, vaguely, toward downtown Los Angeles, but now here it is—the staunch, squat older buildings, the skeletons of newer, taller ones going up—all suffused with the steady white glare of the day, which seems to emanate not so much from the sky down to the earth as from the air itself, as if invisible particles in the ether emitted a steady, slightly foggy phosphorescence. Here is the city, and Laura must either enter it, by way of the left-hand lane, or switch to the right-hand lane and bypass it altogether. If she does that, if she simply continues driving, she'll be headed into the vast, flat stretch of factories and low-rise apartment buildings that surrounds Los Angeles for a hundred miles in every direction. It would be possible to veer right, and find her way eventually to Beverly Hills, or to the beach at Santa Monica, but she doesn't want to shop and she hasn't brought anything for the beach. There is surprisingly little to enter, in this immense bright smoky landscape, and what she wants—someplace private, silent, where she can read, where she can think—is not readily available. If she goes to a store or restaurant, she'll have to perform—she'll have to pretend to need or want something that does not, in any way, interest her. She'll have to move in an orderly fashion; she'll have to examine merchandise and refuse offers of help, or she'll have to sit at a table, order something, consume it, and leave. If she simply parks her car somewhere and sits there, a woman alone, she'll be vulnerable to criminals and to those who'll try to protect her from criminals. She'll be too exposed; she'll look too peculiar.

Even a library would be too public, as would a park.

She pilots her car into the left-hand lane, and drives into the city. She seems to arrive at her decision almost physically, as if by going left she had entered a course of action that was waiting for her as palpably as is Figueroa Street, with its shop windows and shadowed sidewalks. She will check into a hotel. She will say (of course) that she's there for the night, that her husband will be joining her soon. As long as she pays for the room, what's wrong with using it only a couple of hours?

It seems such an extravagant, reckless gesture that she is giddy with the possibility of it, and nervous as a girl. Yes, it's wasteful—a hotel room for an entire night, when all she means to do is sit there reading for two hours or so—but money is not particularly tight right now, and she runs the household with relative thrift. How much can a room cost, really? It can't be that much.

Although she should go to a cheap place—a motel, somewhere on the outskirts—she can't bring herself to. It would feel too illicit; it would feel too sordid. The desk clerk might even take her for some sort of professional; he might ask questions. Motels of that sort are outside her experience, they probably involve codes of conduct with which she's utterly unfamiliar, and so she drives to the Normandy, a sprawling white building just a few blocks away. The Normandy is large, clean, unremarkable. It is V-shaped—twin white ten-story wings that enclose a fountained, urban garden. It has an air of sanitized respectability; it is intended for tourists and businessmen, people whose presence there contains not even the suggestion of mystery. Laura pulls her car up under a chrome canopy on which the hotel's name stands in tall, angular chrome letters. Although it is full daylight, the air under the canopy has a slightly nocturnal quality, a lunar brilliance; a scoured white-on-white clarity. The potted aloe plants on either side of the black glass doors seem astonished to be there.

Laura leaves her car with the attendant, receives her ticket for its redemption, and enters through the heavy glass doors. The lobby is hushed, gelid. A distant chime rings, clear and measured. Laura is at once comforted and unnerved. She walks across the deep blue carpet toward the front desk. This hotel, this lobby, is precisely what she wants—the cool nowhere of it, the immaculate non-smell, the brisk unemotional comings and goings. She feels, immediately, like a citizen of this place. It is so competent, so unconcerned. Still, at the same time, she's here under false or, worse, inexplicable circumstances—she's come, in some obscure way, to escape a cake. She intends to tell the desk clerk that her husband has been unavoidably delayed, and will arrive with their luggage in an hour or so. She has never lied like that before, not to someone she doesn't know or love.

The transaction at the front desk proves surprisingly easy. The clerk, a man about her own age, with a sweet, reedy voice and ravaged skin, clearly not only suspects nothing but does not entertain the possibility of suspicion. When Laura asks, "Have you got a room available?" he simply, unhesitatingly answers, "Yes, we do. Do you need a single or a double?"

"A double," she says. "For my husband and myself. He's coming, with our luggage."

The clerk glances behind her, looking for a man struggling with suitcases. Laura's face burns, but she does not waver.

"He's coming, actually, in an hour or two. He's been delayed, and he sent me on. To see if there's a vacancy."

She touches the black granite countertop to steady herself. Her story, it seems, is wholly implausible. If she and her husband are traveling, why do they have two cars? Why didn't they phone ahead?

The clerk, however, does not flinch. "I'm afraid I've only got rooms on the lower floors. Is that all right?"

"Yes, it's fine. It's just for the one night."

"All right, then. Let's see. Room 19."

Laura signs the registration form with her own name (an invented one would feel too strange, too sordid), pays now ("We may be leaving very early in the morning, we'll be in a terrible hurry, I'd just as soon have it taken care of"). She receives the key.

Leaving the desk, she can hardly believe she's done it. She has gotten the key, passed through the portals. The doors to the elevators, at the far end of the lobby, are hammered bronze, each topped by a horizontal line of brilliant red numerals, and to reach them she passes various arrangements of empty sofas and chairs; the cool slumber of miniature potted palms; and, behind glass, the interior grotto of a combination drugstore and coffee shop, where several solitary men in suits sit with newspapers at the counter, where an older woman in a pale pink waitress costume and a red wig seems to be saying something humorous to no one in particular, and where an almost cartoonishly large lemon-meringue pie, with two slices missing, stands on a pedestal under a clear plastic dome.

Laura rings for the elevator, presses the button for her floor. Under a glass pane on the elevator wall is a photograph of the eggs Benedict that can be ordered in the hotel restaurant until two in the afternoon. She looks at the photograph, thinks about how it is just barely too late to order eggs Benedict. She has been nervous for so long, and her nervousness has not dissipated but its nature seems to have suddenly changed. Her nervousness along with her anger and disappointment in herself are all perfectly recognizable to her but they now reside elsewhere. The decision to check into this hotel, to rise in this elevator, seems to have rescued her the way morphine rescues a cancer patient, not by eradicating the pain but simply by making the pain cease to matter. It's almost as if she's accompanied by an invisible sister, a perverse woman full of rage and recriminations, a woman humiliated by herself, and it is this woman, this unfortunate sister, and not Laura, who needs comfort and silence. Laura could be a nurse, ministering to the pain of another.

She steps out of the elevator, walks calmly down the hall, fits the key into the lock of room 19.

Here is her room, then: a turquoise room, not surprising or unusual in any way, with a turquoise spread on the double bed and a painting (Paris, springtime) in a blond wood frame. The room has a smell, alcohol and pitch pine, bleach, scented soap, all floating heavily over something that is not rancid, not even stale, but not fresh. It is, she thinks, a tired smell. It is the smell of a place that's been used and used.

She goes to the window, parts the filmy white curtains, raises the blinds. There, below, is the V-shaped plaza, with its fountain and struggling rosebushes, its empty stone benches. Again, Laura feels as if she's entered a dream—a dream in which she looks onto this peculiar garden, so uninhabited, at a little past two in the afternoon. She turns from the window. She takes off her shoes. She puts her copy of *Mrs. Dalloway* on the glass-topped night table, and lies on the bed. The room is full of the particular silence that prevails in hotels, a tended silence, utterly unnatural, layered over a substratum of creaks and gurglings, of wheels on carpet.

She is so far away from her life. It was so easy.

It seems, somehow, that she has left her own world and entered the realm of the book. Nothing, of course, could be further from Mrs. Dalloway's London than this turquoise hotel room, and yet she imagines that Virginia Woolf herself, the drowned woman, the genius, might in death inhabit a place not unlike this one. She laughs, quietly, to herself. Please, God, she says silently, let heaven be something better than a room at the Normandy. Heaven would be better furnished, it would be brighter and grander, but it might in fact contain some measure of this hushed remove, this utter absence inside the continuing world. Having this room to herself seems both prim and whorish. She is safe here. She could do anything she wanted to, anything at all. She is somehow like a newlywed, reclining in her chamber, waiting for . . . not her husband, or any other man. For someone. For something.

She reaches for her book. She has marked her place with the silver bookmark ("To My Bookworm, With Love") given her by her husband several birthdays ago.

With a sensation of deep and buoyant release, she begins reading.

She remembered once throwing a sixpence into the Serpentine. But every one remembered; what she loved was this, here, now, in front of her; the fat lady in the cab. Did it matter then, she asked herself, walking toward Bond Street, did it matter that she must inevitably cease completely; all this must go on without her; did she resent it; or did it not become consoling to believe that death ended absolutely? but that somehow on the streets of London, on the ebb and flow of things, here, there, she survived, Peter survived, lived in each other, she being part, she was positive, of the trees at home; of the house there, ugly, rambling all to bits and pieces as it was; part of people she had never met; being laid out like a mist between people she knew best, who lifted her on their branches as she had seen the trees lift the mist, but it spread ever so far, her life, herself. But what was she dreaming as she looked into Hatchards' shop window? What was she trying to recover? What image of white dawn in the country, as she read in the book spread open:

> *Fear no more the heat o' the sun,*
> *Nor the furious winter's rages.*

It is possible to die. Laura thinks, suddenly, of how she—how anyone—can make a choice like that. It is a reckless, vertiginous thought, slightly disembodied—it announces itself inside her head, faintly but distinctly, like a voice crackling from a distant radio station. She could decide to die. It is an abstract, shimmering notion, not particularly morbid. Hotel rooms are where people do things like that, aren't they? It's possible—perhaps even likely—that someone has ended his or her life right here, in this room, on this bed. Someone said, Enough, no more; someone looked for the last time at these white walls, this smooth white ceiling. By going to a hotel, she sees, you leave the particulars of your own life and enter a neutral zone, a clean white room, where dying does not seem quite so strange.

It could, she thinks, be deeply comforting; it might feel so free: to simply go away. To say to them all, I couldn't manage, you had no idea; I didn't want to try anymore. There might, she thinks, be a dreadful beauty in it, like an ice field or a desert in early morning. She could go, as it were, into that other landscape; she could leave them all behind—her child, her husband and Kitty, her parents, everybody—in this battered world (it will never be whole again, it will never be quite clean), saying to one another and to anyone who asks, We thought she was all right, we thought her sorrows were ordinary ones. We had no idea.

She strokes her belly. I would never. She says the words out loud in the clean, silent room: "I would never." She loves life, loves it hopelessly, at least at certain moments; and she would be killing her son as well. She would be killing her son and her husband and the other child, still forming inside her. How could any of them recover from something like that? Nothing she might do as a living wife and mother, no lapse, no fit of rage or depression, could possibly compare. It would be, simply, evil. It would punch a hole in the atmosphere, through which everything she's created—the orderly days, the lighted windows, the table laid for supper—would be sucked away.

Still, she is glad to know (for somehow, suddenly, she knows) that it is possible to stop living. There is comfort in facing the full range of options; in considering all your choices, fearlessly and without guile. She imagines Virginia Woolf, virginal, unbalanced, defeated by the impossible demands of life and art; she imagines her stepping into a river with a stone in her pocket. Laura keeps stroking her belly. It would be as simple, she thinks, as checking into a hotel. It would be as simple as that.

Mrs. Woolf

She sits in the kitchen with Vanessa, drinking her tea.

"There was a lovely coat for Angelica at Harrods," Vanessa says. "But then nothing for the boys, and it seemed so unfair. I suppose I shall give her the coat for her birthday, but then of course she'll be cross because she believes coats ought to come to her anyway, as a matter of course, and not be presented as gifts."

Virginia nods. At the moment, she can't seem to speak. There is so much in the world. There are coats at Harrods; there are children who will be angry and disappointed no matter what one does. There is Vanessa's plump hand on her cup and there is the thrush outside, so beautiful on its pyre; so like millinery.

There is this hour, now, in the kitchen.

Clarissa will not die, not by her own hand. How could she bear to leave all this?

Virginia prepares to offer some wisdom about children. She has scant idea what she'll say, but she will say something.

She would like to say, It is enough. The teacups and the thrush outside, the question of children's coats. It is enough.

Someone else will die. It should be a greater mind than Clarissa's; it should be someone with sorrow and genius enough to turn away from the seductions of the world, its cups and its coats.

"Perhaps Angelica—" Virginia says.

But here's Nelly to the rescue; furious, triumphant, back from London with a parcel containing the China tea and sugared ginger. She holds the package aloft, as if she would hurl it.

"Good afternoon, Mrs. Bell," she says with an executioner's studied calm.

Here is Nelly with the tea and ginger and here, forever, is Virginia, unaccountably happy, better than happy, alive, sitting with Vanessa in the kitchen on an ordinary spring day as Nelly, the subjugated Amazon queen, Nelly the ever indignant, displays what she's been compelled to bring.

Nelly turns away and, although it is not at all their custom, Virginia leans forward and kisses Vanessa on the mouth. It is an innocent kiss, innocent enough, but just now, in this kitchen, behind Nelly's back, it feels like the most delicious and forbidden of pleasures. Vanessa returns the kiss.

Mrs. Dalloway

"Poor Louis."

Julia sighs with a surprisingly elderly mixture of rue and exhausted patience, and she seems, briefly, like a figure of ancient maternal remonstrance; part of a centuries-long line of women who have sighed with rue and exhausted patience over the strange passions of men. Briefly, Clarissa can imagine her daughter at fifty: she will be what people refer to as an ample woman, large of body and spirit, inscrutably capable, decisive, undramatic, an early riser. Clarissa wants, at that moment, to be Louis; not to be *with* him (that can be so thorny, so difficult) but to *be* him, an unhappy person, a strange person, faithless, unscrupulous, loose on the streets.

"Yes," she says. "Poor Louis."

Will Louis spoil the party for Richard? Why did she ask Walter Hardy?

"Such a strange man," Julia says.

"Could you stand it if I gave you a hug?"

Julia laughs, and is nineteen again. She is impossibly beautiful. She goes to movies Clarissa's never heard of, suffers fits of sullenness and elation. She wears six rings on her left hand, none of them the one Clarissa gave her for her eighteenth birthday. She wears a silver ring in her nose.

"Of course," she says.

Clarissa holds Julia, and quickly releases her. "How are you?" she asks again, then instantly regrets it. She worries that it's one of her tics; one of those innocent little habits that inspire thoughts of homicide in an offspring. Her own mother compulsively cleared her throat. Her mother prefaced all contrary opinions by saying, "I hate to be a wet blanket, but—" Those things survive in Clarissa's memory, still capable of inspiring rage, after her mother's kindness and modesty, her philanthropies, have faded. Clarissa says too often to Julia, "How are you?" She does it partly out of nervousness (how can she help being formal with Julia, feeling a little anxious, after all that's happened?), and she does it partly because she wants, simply, to know.

Her party, she thinks, will fail. Richard will be bored and offended, and rightly so. She is superficial; she cares too much about such things. Her daughter must make jokes about it to her friends.

But to have friends like Mary Krull!

"I'm all right," Julia says.

"You look wonderful," Clarissa says in cheerful desperation. At least she's been generous. She's been a mother who compliments her child, gives her confidence, doesn't carp about her own worries.

"Thank you," Julia says. "Did I leave my backpack here yesterday?"

"You did. It's right there on the peg by the door."

"Good. Mary and I are going shopping."

"Where are you meeting her?"

"Actually, she's here. She's outside."

"Oh."

"She's smoking a cigarette."

"Well, maybe when she's finished with her cigarette, she'd like to come in and say hello."

Julia's face darkens with contrition and something else—is her old fury returning? Or is it just ordinary guilt? A silence passes. It seems that some force of conventionality exerts itself, potent as the gravitational pull. Even if you've been defiant all your life; if you've raised a daughter as honorably as you knew how, in a house of women (the father no more than a numbered vial, sorry, Julia, no way of finding him)—even with all that, it seems you find yourself standing one day on a Persian rug, full of motherly disapproval and sour, wounded feelings, facing a girl who despises you (she still must, mustn't she?) for depriving her of a father. *Maybe when she's finished with her cigarette, she'd like to come in and say hello.*

But why shouldn't Mary be held to a few of the fundamental human decencies? You don't wait outside somebody's apartment, no matter how brilliant and furious you are. You enter, and say hello. You get through it.

"I'll get her," Julia says.

"It's all right."

"No, really. She's just out there smoking. You know how she is. There's cigarettes, and then there's everything else."

"Don't haul her in here. Honestly. Go, I set you free."

"No. I want you two to know each other better."

"We know each other perfectly well."

"Don't be afraid, Mother. Mary is a sweetheart. Mary is utterly, utterly harmless."

"I'm not *afraid* of her. For god's sake."

Julia produces an infuriatingly knowing smile, shakes her head, and leaves. Clarissa bends over the coffee table, moves the vase an inch to the left. She has an urge to hide the roses. If only it were someone other than Mary Krull. If it were anyone else.

Julia returns, with Mary in her wake. Here, then, once again, is Mary—Mary the stern and rigorous, Mary the righteous, shaved head beginning to show dark stubble, wearing rat-colored slacks, breasts dangling (she must be past forty) under a ragged white tank top. Here is her heavy tread; here are her knowing, suspicious eyes. Seeing Julia and Mary together, Clarissa thinks of a little girl dragging home a stray dog, all ribs and discolored teeth; a pathetic and ultimately dangerous creature who ostensibly needs a good home but whose hunger in fact runs so deep it cannot be touched by any display of love or bounty. The dog will just keep eating and eating. It will never be satisfied; it will never be tame.

"Hello, Mary," Clarissa says.

"Hey, Clarissa." She strides across the room and pumps Clarissa's hand. Mary's hand is small, strong, surprisingly soft.

"How are you?" Mary asks.

"Fine, thanks. You?"

She shrugs. How *should* I be, how should anyone be, in a world like this? Clarissa has fallen so easily for the trick question. She thinks of her roses. Are children forced to pick them? Do families arrive in fields before dawn and spend their days bent over the bushes, backs aching, fingers bleeding from the thorns?

"Going shopping?" she says, and does not try to hide the contempt in her voice.

Julia says, "New boots. Mary's are about to fall off her feet."

"I hate to shop," Mary says. She offers a hint of an apologetic smile. "It's such a waste of time."

"We're buying boots today," Julia says. "Period."

Clarissa's daughter, this marvelous, intelligent girl, could be some cheerful wife, shepherding her husband through a day of errands. She could be a figure from the fifties, if you made a few relatively minor alterations.

Mary says to Clarissa, "I couldn't do it without help. I can face a cop with tear gas, but don't come near me if you're a sales clerk."

Clarissa realizes, with a shock, that Mary is making an effort. She is trying, in her way, to charm.

"Oh, they can't be that frightening," she says.

"It's stores, it's the whole thing, all that *shit* everywhere, 'scuse me, that *merchandise*, all those *goods*, and ads screaming at you from all over the place, *buy buy buy buy buy,* and when somebody comes up to me with big hair and gobs of makeup on and says, 'Can I help you,' it's all I can do not to scream, 'Bitch, you can't even help *yourself*.' "

"Mm," Clarissa says. "That sounds serious."

Julia says, "Mary, let's go."

Clarissa says to Julia, "Take good care of her."

Fool, Mary Krull thinks. *Smug, self-satisfied witch.*

She corrects herself. Clarissa Vaughan is not the enemy. Clarissa Vaughan is only deluded, neither more nor less than that. She believes that by obeying the rules she can have what men have. She's bought the ticket. It isn't her fault. Still, Mary would like to grab Clarissa's shirtfront and cry out, *You honestly believe that if they come to round up the deviants, they won't stop at your door, don't you? You really are that foolish.*

"Bye, Mother," Julia says.

"Don't forget the backpack," Clarissa says.

"Oh, yes." Julia laughs, and takes her backpack from the peg. It is bright orange canvas, not at all the kind of thing you'd expect her to own.

What, exactly, was wrong with the ring?

Briefly, while Julia's back is turned, Clarissa and Mary face each other. *Fool,* Mary thinks, though she struggles to remain charitable or, at least, serene. No, screw charity. Anything's better than queers of the old school, dressed to pass, bourgeois to the bone, living like husband and wife. Better to be a frank and open asshole, better to be John fucking Wayne, than a well-dressed dyke with a respectable job.

Fraud, Clarissa thinks. You've fooled my daughter, but you don't fool me. I know a conquistador when I see one. I know all about making a splash. It isn't hard. If you shout loud enough, for long enough, a crowd will gather to see what all the noise is about. It's the nature of crowds. They don't stay long, unless you give them reason. You're just as bad as most men, just that aggressive, just that self-aggrandizing, and your hour will come and go.

"All right," Julia says. "Let's go."

Clarissa says, "Remember the party. At five."

"Sure," Julia answers. She hoists her bright orange backpack over her shoulder, causing Clarissa and Mary to suffer through a moment of identical feeling. Each adores with particular force Julia's brisk and kindly self-assurance, the limitless days that lie ahead.

"See you," Clarissa says.

She is trivial. She is someone who thinks too much about parties. If only Julia can someday forgive her . . .

"Bye," says Mary, and she strides, in Julia's wake, out the door.

But why Mary Krull, of all people? Why should a straight girl like Julia make herself an acolyte? Is she still this anxious for a father?

Mary lingers a moment behind Julia, allowing herself a view of Julia's broad, graceful back, the twin moons of her ass. Mary is almost overwhelmed by desire and by something else, a subtler and more exquisitely painful nerve that branches through her desire. Julia inspires in her an erotic patriotism, as if Julia were the distant country in which Mary was born and from which she has been expelled.

"Come on," Julia calls cheerfully over her shoulder, over the synthetic orange brilliance of her backpack.

Mary stands for a moment, watching. She believes she has never seen anything so beautiful. *If you could love me,* she thinks, *I'd do anything. Do you understand? Anything.*

"Come *on,*" Julia calls again, and Mary hurries after her, hopelessly, in agony (Julia does not love her, not like that, and never will), on her way to buy new boots.

Mrs. Woolf

Vanessa and the children are gone, back to Charleston. Nelly is downstairs preparing dinner, mysteriously cheerful, more so than she's been in days—is it possible that she appreciates having been ordered out on a foolish errand, that she so savors the injustice of it she's inspired to sing in the kitchen? Leonard is writing in his study, and the thrush lies on its bed of grass and roses in the garden. Virginia stands at a parlor window, watching the dark descend on Richmond.

It is the close of an ordinary day. On her writing stand in an unlit room lie the pages of the new novel, about which she cherishes extravagant hopes and which, at this moment, she fears (she believes she *knows*) will prove arid and weak, devoid of true feeling; a dead end. It has been only a few hours, and yet what she felt in the kitchen with Vanessa—that potent satisfaction, that blessedness—has so utterly evaporated it might never have occurred. There is only this: the smell of Nelly's beef boiling (revolting, and Leonard will watch as she struggles to eat it), all the clocks in the house about to strike the half hour, her own face becoming more and more strongly reflected in the window glass as the streetlamps—pale lemon against an ink-blue sky—light up all over Richmond. It is enough, she tells herself. She strives to believe that. It is enough to be in this house, delivered from the war, with a night's reading ahead of her, and then sleep, and then work again in the morning. It is enough that the streetlamps throw yellow shadows into the trees.

She can feel the headache creeping up the back of her neck. She stiffens. No, it's the memory of the headache, it's her fear of the headache, both of them so vivid as to be at least briefly indistinguishable from an onset of the headache itself. She stands erect, waiting. It's all right. It's all right. The walls of the room do not waver; nothing murmurs from within the plaster. She is herself, standing here, with a husband at home, with servants and rugs and pillows and lamps. She is herself.

She knows she will leave almost before she decides to leave. A walk; she will simply take a walk. She will be back in half an hour, or less. Quickly she puts on her cloak and hat, her scarf. She goes quietly to the back door, steps out, shuts it carefully behind her. She would prefer that no one ask where she's going, or when she can be expected back.

Outside, in the garden, is the shadowy mound of the thrush on its bier, sheltered by the hedges. A strong wind has blown in from the east, and Virginia shudders. It seems that she has left the house (where beef is boiling, where lamps are lit) and entered the realm of the dead bird. She thinks of how the newly buried remain all night in their graves, after the mourners have recited prayers, laid down wreaths, and returned to the village. After the wheels have rolled away over the dried mud of the road, after the suppers have been eaten and the bedcovers drawn down; after all that has happened the grave remains, its flowers tossed lightly by the wind. It is frightening but not entirely disagreeable, this cemetery feeling. It is real; it is all but overwhelmingly real. It is, in its way, more bearable, nobler, right now, than the beef and the lamps. She descends the stairs, walks out onto the grass.

The body of the thrush is still there (odd, how the neighborhood cats and dogs are not interested), tiny even for a bird, so utterly unalive, here in the dark, like a lost glove, this little empty handful of death. Virginia stands over it. It's rubbish now; it has shed the beauty of the afternoon just as Virginia has shed her tea-table wonder over cups and coats; just as the day is shedding its warmth. In the morning Leonard will scoop bird and grass and roses up with a shovel, and throw them all out. She thinks of how much more space a being occupies in life than it does in death; how much illusion of size is contained in gestures and movements, in breathing. Dead, we are revealed in our true dimensions, and they are surprisingly modest. Hadn't her own mother seemed to have been removed surreptitiously and replaced by a littler version made of pale iron? Hadn't she, Virginia, felt in herself an empty space, surprisingly small, where it seemed strong feeling ought to reside?

Here, then, is the world (house, sky, a first tentative star) and here is its opposite, this small dark shape in a circle of roses. It's rubbish, that's all. Beauty and dignity were illusions fostered by the company of children, sustained for the benefit of children.

She turns and walks away. It seems possible, at this moment, that there is somewhere else—a place having to do neither with boiled beef nor with the circle of roses. She passes through the garden gate and into the passageway, heads toward town.

As she crosses Princes Street and goes down Waterloo Place (toward what?) she passes others: a plump, stately man with a satchel, two women who must be servants returning from an afternoon off, chattering, white legs flashing from under thin coats, the cheap glint of a bracelet. Virginia gathers the collar of her cloak around her neck, though it isn't cold. It is merely darkening, with a wind. She believes she will walk into town, yes, but what will she do there? The shops, even now, are being swept and readied for closing. She passes a couple, a man and woman younger than herself, walking together, leisurely, bent toward each other in the soft lemon-colored glow of a streetlamp, talking (she hears the man say, "told me *something something something* in this establishment, *something something,* harrumph, indeed"); both man and woman wearing stylish hats, the fringed end of a mustard scarf (whose?) rippling behind like a flag; both of them bent slightly forward as well as toward each other, mounting the hill, holding their hats against the wind, avid but unhurried, coming home (most likely) from a day in London, he saying now, "And so I must ask you," after which he lowers his voice—Virginia can't make out the words at all—and the woman emits a gleeful little shriek, showing a quick white flash of tooth, and the man laughs, striding forward, setting down with perfect confidence the toe of one and then another perfectly polished brown shoe.

I am alone, Virginia thinks, as the man and woman continue up the hill and she continues down. She is, of course, not alone, not in a way anyone else would recognize, and yet at this moment, walking through wind toward the lights of the Quadrant, she can feel the nearness of the old devil (what else to call it?), and she knows she will be utterly alone if and when the devil chooses to appear again. The devil is a headache; the devil is a voice inside a wall; the devil is a fin breaking through dark waves. The devil is the brief, twittering nothing that was a thrush's life. The devil sucks all the beauty from the world, all the hope, and what remains when the devil has finished is a realm of the living dead—joyless, suffocating. Virginia feels, right now, a certain tragic grandeur, for the devil is many things but he is not petty, not sentimental; he seethes with a lethal, intolerable truth. Right now, walking, free of her headache, free of the voices, she can face the devil, but she must keep walking, she must not turn back.

When she reaches the Quadrant (the butcher and greengrocer have already rolled up their awnings) she turns toward the rail station. She will go, she thinks, to London; she will simply go to London, like Nelly on her errand, although Virginia's errand will be the trip itself, the half hour on the train, the disembarking at Paddington Station, the possibility of walking down a street into another street, and another after that. What a lark! What a plunge! It seems that she can survive, she can prosper, if she has London around her; if she disappears for a while into the enormity of it, brash and brazen now under a sky empty of threat, all the uncurtained windows (here a woman's grave profile, there the crown of a carved chair), the traffic, men and women going lightly by in evening clothes; the smells of wax and petrol, of perfume, as someone, somewhere (on one of these broad avenues, in one of these white, porticoed houses), plays a piano; as horns bleat and dogs bay, as the whole raucous carnival turns and turns, blazing, shimmering; as Big Ben strikes the hours, which fall in leaden circles over the partygoers and the omnibuses, over stone Queen Victoria seated before the Palace on her shelves of geraniums, over the parks that lie sunken in their shadowed solemnity behind black iron fences.

Virginia descends the stairs to the rail station. The Richmond station is at once a portal and a destination. It is columned, canopied, full of a faint burnt smell, slightly desolate even when crowded (as it is now), lined with yellow wooden benches that do not encourage lingering. She checks the clock, sees that a train has just pulled away and the next will not leave for almost twenty-five minutes. She stiffens. She had imagined (foolish!) stepping straight onto a train or, at most, waiting five or ten minutes. She stands impatiently before the clock, then walks a few slow paces down the platform. If she does this, if she gets on the train that leaves in, what now, twenty-three minutes, and goes to London, and walks in London, and catches the last train back (that will get her home to Richmond at ten minutes past eleven), Leonard will be insane with worry. If she calls him (there is a public telephone, recently installed, here at the station) he'll be furious, he'll demand that she return immediately; he'll suggest (he would never say it outright) that if she becomes exhausted and overwhelmed, if she falls ill again, she will have brought it on herself. And here, of course, is the dilemma: he's entirely right and horribly wrong at the same time. She is better, she is safer, if she rests in Richmond; if she does not speak too much, write too much, feel too much; if she does not travel impetuously to London and walk through its streets; and yet she is dying this way, she is gently dying on a bed of roses. Better, really, to face the fin in the water than to live in hiding, as if the war were still on (strange, how the first memory that springs to mind, after all that, is the endless waiting in the cellar, the whole household crammed in together, and having to make conversation for hours with Nelly and Lottie). Her life (already past forty!) is being measured away, cupful by cupful, and the carnival wagon that bears Vanessa—the whole gaudy party of her, that vast life, the children and paints and lovers, the brilliantly cluttered house—has passed on into the night, leaving its echo of cymbals behind, its accordion notes, as wheels roll off down the road. No, she will not telephone from the station, she will do it once she's reached London, once there's nothing to be done. She will take her punishment.

She buys a ticket from the red-faced man behind the grille. She goes and sits, very erect, on a wooden bench. Eighteen minutes still. She sits on the bench, staring straight ahead (if only she had something to read) until she can't bear it any longer (fifteen minutes still). She stands and walks back out of the station. If she strolls to the corner along Kew Road, and strolls back, she will be just in time for her train.

She is passing her fragmented golden reflection in the gold name of the butcher shop, suspended on the glass over a lamb's carcass (a tuft of pale wool still clings to its anklebone), when she sees Leonard walking toward her. She thinks, for a moment, that she will turn and run back to the station; she thinks she will escape some sort of catastrophe. She does not do any such thing. She continues walking forward, toward Leonard, who has clearly come out in a hurry, still wearing his leather slippers, and who looks exceedingly thin—gaunt—in his vest and corduroy jacket, his open collar. Although he has come after her like a constable or proctor, a figure of remonstrance, she is impressed by how small he seems, in slippers on Kew Road; how middle-aged and ordinary. She sees him, briefly, as a stranger might see him: merely another of the many men who walk on streets. She is sad for him, and strangely moved. She manages an ironic smile.

"Mr. Woolf," she says. "What an unexpected pleasure."

He says, "Would you like to tell me what you're doing, please?"

"I'm taking a walk. Does it seem mysterious?"

"Only when you vanish from the house, just before dinner, without a word."

"I didn't like to interrupt you. I knew you were working."

"I was."

"Well, then."

"You mustn't disappear. I don't like it."

"Leonard, you're acting very oddly."

He scowls. "Am I? I don't know what it is, really. I went to look for you, and you weren't there. I thought, something's happened. I don't know why."

She imagines him searching the house for her, checking the garden. She thinks of him rushing out, past the body of the thrush, through the gate, down the hill. She is suddenly, immensely sorry for him. She should, she knows, tell him that his premonition was not entirely wrong; that she had in fact staged an escape of sorts, and had in fact meant to disappear, if only for a few hours.

"Nothing's happened," she says. "Just an airing along the avenues. It's such a night."

"I was so worried," he says. "I don't know why."

They stand together in a brief, unaccustomed silence. They look into the window of the butcher's shop, where they are reflected, brokenly, in the golden letters.

Leonard says, "We must go back for Nelly's joint. We have approximately fifteen minutes before she goes on a rampage and burns the house down."

Virginia hesitates. But London! She still wants, desperately, to get on the train.

"You must be hungry," she says.

"I am, a bit. You surely are, too."

She thinks suddenly of how frail men are; how full of terror. She thinks of Quentin, going into the house to wash the thrush's death off his hands. It seems, at that moment, that she straddles an invisible line, one foot on this side, the other on that. On this side is stern, worried Leonard, the row of closed shops, the dark rise that leads back to Hogarth House, where Nelly waits impatiently, almost gleefully, for her chance at further grievances. On the other side is the train. On the other side is London, and all London implies about freedom, about kisses, about the possibilities of art and the sly dark glitter of madness. Mrs. Dalloway, she thinks, is a house on a hill where a party is about to begin; death is the city below, which Mrs. Dalloway loves and fears and which she wants, in some way, to walk into so deeply she will never find her way back again.

Virginia says, "It's time for us to move back to London. Don't you think?"

"I'm not at all sure," he answers.

"I've been better for a long while now. We can't haunt the suburbs forever, can we?"

"Let's discuss it over dinner, shall we?"

"All right, then."

"Do you want so much to live in London?" he asks.

"I do," she says. "I wish it were otherwise. I wish I were happy with the quiet life."

"As do I."

"Come along," she says.

She keeps the ticket in her bag. She will never mention to Leonard that she'd planned on fleeing, even for a few hours. As if he were the one in need of care and comfort—as if he were the one in danger—Virginia links her arm in his, and gives his elbow an affectionate squeeze. They start up the hill to Hogarth House, arm in arm, like any middle-aged couple going home.

Mrs. Dalloway

"More coffee?" Oliver says to Sally.

"Thanks." Sally hands her coffee cup to Oliver's assistant, a surprisingly plain young man, white-blond, hollow-cheeked, who, although presented as an assistant, seems to be in charge of pouring coffee. Sally had expected an impeccable young stud, all jaw and biceps. This weedy, eager boy would look right at home behind the perfume counter in a department store.

"So what do you think?" Oliver says.

Sally watches her coffee being poured, to avoid looking at Oliver. When the cup has been set in front of her she glances at Walter Hardy, who betrays nothing. Walter has a talent, remarkable in its way, for looking utterly attentive and entirely blank, like a lizard that has crawled onto a sunny rock.

"Interesting," Sally says.

"Yes," Oliver answers.

Sally nods judiciously, sips her coffee. "I wonder," she says, "if it could actually get made."

"I think it's time," Oliver answers. "I think people are ready."

"Do you, really?"

Sally appeals, silently, to Walter. *Speak, you moron.* Walter simply nods, blinking, basking, alert to the possibility of danger and, at the same time, all but hypnotized by the heat that emanates from Oliver St. Ives, who is trim and rumpled, forty-five-ish, keen-eyed behind his modest gold-rimmed glasses; whose image on celluloid has survived countless attempts by other men to murder him, swindle him, blacken his name, ruin his family; who has made love to goddesses, always with the same abashed ardor, as if he can't believe his luck.

"Yes," Oliver says, with an audible rise of impatience in his voice.

"It sounds really, well, interesting," Sally says, and can't help laughing.

"Walter could do it," Oliver says. "Walter could pull it off. Definitely."

At the sound of his name Walter rouses, blinks more rapidly, shifts forward in his chair, all but changes color. "I'd love to take a crack at it," he says.

Oliver smiles his famous smile. Sally is still surprised, sometimes, at how much Oliver resembles himself. Aren't movie stars supposed to be short, ordinary, and ill-tempered? Don't they owe us that? Oliver St. Ives must have been identifiable as a movie star since childhood. He is incandescent; he is Bunyanesque. He can't be much under six foot four, and his perfectly formed, blond-tufted hands could easily palm most other men's heads. He is large-featured, flat-faced, and if in person he is not quite so handsome as he is on screen he carries every bit as much of that mysterious and undeniable singularity, a singularity not just of spirit but of the flesh as well, as if all other brawny, exuberant, unflinching American men were somehow copies of him, either well or indifferently made.

"Do," Oliver says to Walter. "I have great faith in your powers. Hey, you wrecked my career with one little story."

Walter tries a knowing grin but it comes out hideously debased, and full of hatred. Sally imagines him, suddenly and with perfect clarity, at the age of ten. He would have been overweight, desperately friendly, able to calibrate the social standing of other ten-year-olds to the millimeter. He would have been capable of treachery in almost any form.

"Don't give me that," Walter says, grinning. "Didn't I try to talk you out of it? How many times did I call?"

"Oh, don't worry, little friend, I'm pulling your leg," Oliver says. "I don't regret anything, not one thing. What do you think about the screenplay?"

"I've never tried a thriller before," Walter says.

"It's easy. It's the easiest thing in the world. Rent a half dozen of the ones that made money, you'll know all you need to know."

"This one would be a little different, though," Sally says.

"No," Oliver answers with smiling, peevish patience. "No

different. This one would have a gay man for a hero. That's the only thing, and it's not that big a deal. He wouldn't be tortured about his sexuality. He wouldn't have HIV. He'd just be a gay guy who does his job. Who saves the world, one way or another."

"Mm-hm," Walter says. "I think I could do that. I'd like to try."

"Good. Excellent."

Sally sips her coffee, wanting to be gone, wanting to stay; wanting not to want to be admired by Oliver St. Ives. There is no more powerful force in the world, she thinks, than fame. To help maintain her equilibrium she looks around the apartment, which appeared on the cover of *Architectural Digest* a year before Oliver revealed himself and will probably not appear in a magazine ever again, given what Oliver's announced sexual nature now implies about his taste. The irony, Sally thinks, is that the apartment is hideous in a way she associates with macho flamboyance, with its Lucite coffee table and brown lacquered walls, its niches in which spotlit Asian and African objects (Oliver surely thinks of them as "dramatically lit") suggest, despite their immaculate and reverential display, not so much connoisseurship as plunder. This is the third time Sally has been here, and each time she's felt the urge to confiscate the treasures and return them to their rightful owners. She feigns attention to Oliver while imagining herself entering a remote mountain village amid cheers and ululations, carrying the age-blackened antelope mask or the pale green, faintly phosphorescent porcelain bowl in which two painted carp have swum for ten centuries.

"You're not so sure, Sal?" Oliver says.

"Hm?"

"You're not convinced."

"Oh, well, convinced, not convinced, I'm way out of my depth here. What do I know about Hollywood?"

"You're smarter than most of those characters out there. You're one of the only people connected with the business who I respect."

"I'm not 'connected with the business,' not at all, you know what I do—"

"You're not convinced."

"Well, no, I'm not," she says. "But really, who cares?"

Oliver sighs and pushes his glasses higher up on his nose, a gesture Sally is certain she remembers from one of the movies, something involving a mild-mannered (accountant? attorney? could it have been a TV producer?) who is finally driven to brutally extinguish a small army of drug dealers to save his teenage daughter.

"I admit we'd have to do it just right," Oliver says slowly. "I don't have any illusions about it being a sure thing."

"Would he have a lover?"

"A companion. A sidekick. Sort of like Batman and Robin."

"Would they have sex?"

"Nobody has sex in a thriller. It slows the action down too much. You lose the kids. At most, there's a kiss at the end."

"Would they kiss at the end, then?"

"That's Walter's department."

"Walter?"

Walter blinks back into action. "Hey," he says, "I just three minutes ago said I think maybe I could do it. Don't get too fancy on me, huh?"

Oliver says, "We can't be calculating about this. I've seen too many people sit down to write a surefire hit, and they always bomb. There's some kind of jinx."

"You think people would be interested?" Sally says. "I mean, enough people?"

Oliver sighs again, and this sigh is markedly different in tone from the previous one. This is a resigned and final sigh, running toward the nasal register, meaningful in its lack of drama. It is like the first disinterested sigh a lover sends over the telephone wires, the sigh that signals the earliest beginning of the end. Has Oliver used that sigh in a movie? Or has someone else, somebody real, sighed like that into Sally's ear long ago?

"Well," Oliver says. He places his hands, palms down, on the tablecloth. "Walter, why don't you and I talk in a couple of days, after you've had a chance to mull this over."

"Sure," Walter says. "Sounds good."

Sally takes a last sip of her coffee. It is, of course, a man's game; a man's body of delusion. They never needed her in the first place, not really. After he appeared on her show Oliver just got the idea (and let's face it, he's no Einstein) that Sally was his muse and mentor, some sort of Sappho speaking rueful wisdoms from her island. Better to put a stop to that right now.

Still, there is this terrible desire to be loved by Oliver St. Ives. Still, there is this horror at being left behind.

"Thanks for coming," Oliver says, and Sally conquers an urge to recant—to lean toward Oliver over the table, over the wreckage of lunch, and say, *I've thought it over, and I think a thriller with a gay hero could really work.*

Goodbye, then. Time to return to the streets.

Sally stands with Walter on the corner of Madison and Seventieth. They do not talk about Oliver St. Ives. They understand, variously, that Walter has succeeded and Sally has failed, and that Sally has succeeded and Walter failed. They find other things to talk about.

"I guess I'll see you tonight," Walter says.

"Mm-hm," Sally answers. Who invited Walter?

"How *is* Richard," Walter asks. He ducks his head awkwardly, reverently, pointing the bill of his cap down toward the cigarette butts and gray circles of chewing gum, the wadded wrapper which, Sally can't help noticing, is from a Quarter Pounder. She's never had a Quarter Pounder.

The light changes. They cross.

"All right," Sally says. "Well. Pretty sick."

"These times," Walter says. "God, these times."

Sally is taken, again, by a wave of indignation that rises up under her belly and washes her vision with heat. It's Walter's vanity that's unbearable. It's knowing that as he says the correct and respectful things—even as he quite possibly *feels* the correct and respectful things—he's thinking, too, of how fine it is to be the semifamous novelist Walter Hardy, friend to movie stars and poets, still healthy and muscular past the age of forty. He would be more comic if he had less influence in the world.

"Well," Sally says on the far corner, but before she can take her leave Walter strides up to a store window and stands with his face several inches from the glass.

"Look at these," he says. "How beautiful."

There in the window are three silk shirts, each displayed on a plaster reproduction of a classical Greek statue. One shirt is pale apricot, another emerald, the third a deep, royal blue. Each is differently embroidered along the collar and down the front in silver fine as a spider's thread. All three hang liquidly, iridescently, over the statues' lean torsos, and from each collar emerges a serene white head with full lips, a straight nose, and blank white eyes.

"Mm," Sally says. "Yes. Beautiful."

"Maybe I'll get one for Evan. He could use a present today. Come on."

Sally hesitates, then follows Walter into the store, unwillingly, helplessly borne by an unexpected surge of remorse. Yes, Walter is ridiculous, but along with her disdain Sally seems to feel an awful and unavoidable tenderness for the poor fuck, who has spent the last few years expecting his pretty, brainless boyfriend, his trophy, to die and now, suddenly, is faced with the prospect (does he have mixed feelings?) of the boyfriend's survival. Death and resurrection are always mesmerizing, Sally thinks, and it doesn't seem to matter much whether they involve the hero, the villain, or the clown.

The store is all varnished maple and black granite. It has somehow been made to smell faintly of eucalyptus. Shirts are laid out on the glossy black countertops.

"I think the blue," Walter says as they enter. "Blue's a good color for Evan."

Sally lets Walter speak to the handsome young clerk with the slicked-back hair. She wanders meditatively among the shirts, looks at the tag on a cream-colored shirt with mother-of-pearl buttons. It costs four hundred dollars. Is it pathetic, she wonders, or heroic to buy a fabulous, hideously expensive new shirt for your tentatively recovering lover. Is it both? Sally herself has never developed the knack for buying gifts for Clarissa. Even after all these years, she can't be sure what Clarissa will like. There have been successes—the chocolate-colored cashmere scarf last Christmas, the antique lacquered box in which she keeps her letters—but there have been at least as many failures. There was the extravagant watch from Tiffany's (too formal, it seems), the yellow sweater (was it the color or the neck?), the black leather handbag (just wrong, impossible to say why). Clarissa refuses to admit it when a gift doesn't please her, despite Sally's exhortations. Every present, according to Clarissa, is perfect, exactly what she'd hoped for, and all the hapless giver can do is wait and see whether the watch will be deemed "too good for everyday," or the sweater be worn once, to an obscure party, and never appear again. Sally begins to be angry with Clarissa, Walter Hardy, and Oliver St. Ives; with every optimistic, dishonest living being; but then she glances over at Walter in the process of buying his lover's brilliant blue shirt, and is filled instead with longing. Clarissa is probably at home right now.

Sally suddenly, urgently wants to get home. She says to Walter, "I've got to go. It's later than I thought."

"I won't be long," Walter says.

"I'm off. See you later."

"You like the shirt?"

Sally fingers the fabric, which is supple and minutely grained, vaguely fleshly. "I love it," she says. "It's a wonderful shirt."

The clerk smiles gratefully, shyly, as if he were personally responsible for the shirt's beauty. He is not aloof or condescending, as you might expect of a handsome boy working in a store like this. Where do they come from, these impeccable beauties who work as salesclerks? For what do they hope?

"Yes," Walter says. "It's a great shirt, isn't it?"

"Goodbye."

"Hey. See you later."

Sally gets out of the store as quickly as she can, marches toward the subway at Sixty-eighth. She'd like to come home with a gift for Clarissa, but can't imagine what. She'd like to tell Clarissa something, something important, but can't get it phrased. "I love you" is easy enough. "I love you" has become almost ordinary, being said not only on anniversaries and birthdays but spontaneously, in bed or at the kitchen sink or even in cabs within hearing of foreign drivers who believe women should walk three paces behind their husbands. Sally and Clarissa are not stingy with their affections, and that of course is good, but now Sally finds that she wants to go home and say something more, something that extends not only beyond the sweet and the comforting but beyond passion itself. What she wants to say has to do with all the people who've died; it has to do with her own feelings of enormous good fortune and imminent, devastating loss. If anything happens to Clarissa she, Sally, will go on living but she will not, exactly, survive. She will not be all right. What she wants to say has to do not only with joy but with the penetrating, constant fear that is joy's other half. She can bear the thought of her own death but cannot bear the thought of Clarissa's. This love of theirs, with its reassuring domesticity and its easy silences, its permanence, has yoked Sally directly to the machinery of mortality itself. Now there is a loss beyond imagining. Now there is a cord she can follow from this moment, walking toward the subway on the Upper East Side, through tomorrow and the next day and the next, all the way to the end of her life and the end of Clarissa's.

She rides the subway downtown, stops at the flower stand attached to the Korean market on the corner. It's the usual array, carnations and mums, a scattering of gaunt lilies, freesia, daisies, bunches of hothouse tulips in white, yellow, and red, their petals going leathery at the tips. Zombie flowers, she thinks; just product, forced into being like chickens whose feet never touch ground from egg to slaughter. Sally stands frowning before the flowers on their graduated wooden platforms, sees herself and the flowers reflected in the mirror tiles at the back of the cooler (there she is, gray-haired, sharp-faced, sallow [how did she grow so old?], she's got to get more sun, really), and thinks there is nothing in the world she wants for herself or Clarissa, not four-hundred-dollar shirts, not these pitiful flowers, not anything. She is about to leave empty-handed when she notices a single bouquet of yellow roses in a brown rubber bucket in the corner. They are just beginning to open. Their petals, at the base, are suffused with a deeper yellow, almost orange, a mango-colored blush that spreads upward and diffuses itself in hairline veins. They so convincingly resemble real flowers, grown from earth in a garden, that they seem to have gotten into the cooler by mistake. Sally buys them quickly, almost furtively, as if she fears the Korean woman who runs the stand will realize there's been a mix-up and inform her, gravely, that these roses are not for sale. She walks along Tenth Street with the roses in her hand, feeling exultant, and when she enters the apartment she is slightly aroused. How long has it been since they've had sex?

"Hey," she calls. "Are you home?"

"In here," Clarissa answers, and Sally can tell from her voice that something's wrong. Is she about to walk into one of those little ambushes that pepper their life together? Has she stepped, with her bouquet and her nascent desire, into a scene of domestic peevishness, the world gone gray and morbid because she has once again revealed her selfishness and left something undone, failed to clean something, forgotten some important call? Her joy fades; her lust evaporates. She walks into the living room with the roses.

"What's up?" she says to Clarissa, who is sitting on the sofa, just sitting there, as if she were in a doctor's waiting room. She looks at Sally with a peculiar expression, more disoriented than stricken, as if she is not quite sure who she is, and Sally briefly experiences an intimation of the decline to come. If they both survive long enough, if they stay together (and how, after all this, could they part?), they will watch each other fade.

"Nothing," she says.

"Are you all right?"

"Hm? Oh, yes. I don't know. Louis is in town. He's come back."

"Bound to happen eventually."

"He stopped by, just rang the buzzer. We talked for a while, and then he started crying."

"Really?"

"Yes. Out of nowhere, more or less. Then Julia came over, and he ran off."

"Louis. What can you say?"

"He's dating a new boy. A student."

"Right. Well."

"And then Julia turned up with Mary—"

"My god. The whole circus has been here."

"Oh, look, Sally. You brought roses."

"What? Oh, well. Yes."

Sally flourishes the roses and, at the same moment, notices the vase full of roses Clarissa has put on the table. They both laugh.

"This is sort of an O. Henry moment, isn't it?" Sally says.

"You can't possibly have too many roses," Clarissa says.

Sally hands the flowers to her and for a moment they are both simply and entirely happy. They are present, right now, and they have managed, somehow, over the course of eighteen years, to continue loving each other. It is enough. At this moment, it is enough.

Mrs. Brown

She is later than she'd meant to be, but not seriously late; not so late as to need an explanation. It is almost six. She has gotten halfway through the book. Driving to Mrs. Latch's house, she is full of what she's read: Clarissa and insane Septimus, the flowers, the party. Images drift through her mind: the figure in the car, the airplane with its message. Laura occupies a twilight zone of sorts; a world composed of London in the twenties, of a turquoise hotel room, and of this car, driving down this familiar street. She is herself and not herself. She is a woman in London, an aristocrat, pale and charming, a little false; she is Virginia Woolf; and she is this other, the inchoate, tumbling thing known as herself, a mother, a driver, a swirling streak of pure life like the Milky Way, a friend of Kitty (whom she's kissed, who may be dying), a pair of hands with coral-colored fingernails (one chipped) and a diamond wedding band gripping the wheel of a Chevrolet as a pale blue Plymouth taps its brake lights ahead of her, as late-afternoon summer sun assumes its golden depths, as a squirrel dashes across a telephone wire, its tail a pale gray question mark.

She pulls up in front of Mrs. Latch's house, where two painted plaster squirrels are attached to the gable over the garage. She gets out of her car and stands for a moment, looking up at the plaster squirrels, still holding her car keys. Beside her, the car emits a peculiar ticking sound (it's been doing this for several days now, she'll have to take it by the mechanic's). She is overtaken by a sensation of unbeing. There is no other word for it. Standing beside her ticking car, facing Mrs. Latch's garage (the plaster squirrels throw long shadows), she is no one; she is nothing. It seems, briefly, that by going to the hotel she has slipped out of her life, and this driveway, this garage, are utterly strange to her. She has been away. She has been thinking kindly, even longingly, of death. It comes to her here, in Mrs. Latch's driveway—she has been thinking longingly of death. She has gone to a hotel in secret, the way she might go to meet a lover. She stands, holding her car keys and her purse, staring at Mrs. Latch's garage. The door, painted white, has a little green-shuttered window in it, as if the garage were a miniature house attached to the larger house. Laura's breathing is suddenly labored. She's slightly dizzy—it seems she might stumble and collapse onto Mrs. Latch's smooth concrete drive. She considers getting back into her car, and driving away again. She forces herself to go forward. She reminds herself: she has to retrieve her child, take him home, and finish assembling her husband's birthday dinner. She has to do those ordinary things.

With some effort, she draws a breath and goes up the walk to Mrs. Latch's narrow front porch. It's the secrecy, she tells herself; it's the strangeness of what she's just done, though there's no real harm in it, is there? She's *not* meeting a lover, like some wife from a cheap romance. She simply went away for a few hours, read her book, and came back. It's a secret only because she can't quite think how she'd explain, well, any of it—the kiss, the cake, the panicky moment when her car topped Chavez Ravine. She certainly doesn't know how she'd explain two and a half hours spent reading in a rented room.

She draws another breath. She rings Mrs. Latch's rectangular, illuminated doorbell, which glows orange in the late-afternoon sun.

Mrs. Latch opens the door almost immediately, as if she'd been standing right there, waiting. Mrs. Latch is florid, huge-hipped in Bermuda shorts, overly kind; her house is full of a rich brown smell, some sort of meat roasting, which unfurls from behind her when she opens the door.

"Well, hello," she says.

"Hi," Laura answers. "Sorry I'm late."

"Not at all. We've been having a fine time. Come on in."

Richie rushes in from the living room. He is flushed, alarmed, all but overwhelmed by love and relief. There is the feeling that Laura has caught him and Mrs. Latch at something; the feeling that they've both stopped what they were doing and hurriedly stashed some sort of evidence. No, she has a guilty conscience today; it's just, she thinks, that he's confused. He's spent the last few hours in another realm altogether. Staying at

Mrs. Latch's house, even for a few hours, he has begun losing track of his own life. He has begun to believe, and not happily, that he lives here, has perhaps always lived here, amid this massive yellow furniture, these grass-cloth-covered walls.

Richie breaks into tears and runs toward her.

"Oh, now," Laura says, picking him up. She inhales his smell, the deep essence of him, a profound cleanliness, undefinable. Holding him, inhaling, she feels better.

"He's glad to see you," Mrs. Latch says with elaborately hearty, bitter good cheer. Had she imagined she was some kind of treat for him, a favorite, and her house a house of marvels? Yes, she probably had. Does she suddenly resent him for being a momma's boy? She probably does.

"Hey there, Bug," Laura says, close to her son's small pink ear. She is proud of her maternal calm, her claim on the boy. She is embarrassed by his tears. Do people think she's overprotective? Why does he do this so often?

"Did you get it all done?" Mrs. Latch asks.

"Yes. More or less. Thanks so much for taking him."

"Oh, we had a fine time together," she says heartily, angrily. "You can bring him by any time."

"Did you have fun?" Laura asks.

"Uh-huh," Richie says, his tears abating. His face is a miniature agony of hope, sorrow, and confusion.

"Were you good?"

He nods.

"Did you miss me?"

"Yes!" he says.

"Well, I had a lot to do," Laura says. "We have to give your daddy a proper birthday tonight, don't we?"

He nods. He continues staring at her with teary, abashed suspicion, as if she might not be his mother at all.

Laura pays Mrs. Latch, accepts a bird of paradise from her yard. Mrs. Latch always offers something—a flower, cookies—as if that were the object of payment, and the babysitting were free. Laura, apologizing again for her tardiness, citing her husband's imminent arrival, cuts short the customary fifteen-minute conversation, puts Richie in the car, and pulls away with a last, slightly exaggerated wave. Her three ivory bangles click together.

Once they are away from Mrs. Latch, Laura says to Richie, "Boy oh boy, we're in trouble now. We've got to race right home and get that dinner started. We should have been there an hour ago."

He nods solemnly. The weight and grain of life reassert themselves; the nowhere feeling vanishes. This moment, now, midblock, as the car approaches a stop sign, is unexpectedly large and still, serene—Laura enters it the way she might enter a church from a noisy street. On either side, sprinklers throw brilliant cones of mist up over the lawns. Late sun gilds an aluminum carport. It is unutterably real. She knows herself as a wife and mother, pregnant again, driving home, as veils of water are tossed up into the air.

Richie doesn't speak. He watches her. Laura brakes for the stop sign. She says, "It's a good thing Daddy works as late as he does. We'll put it all together in time, don't you think so?"

She glances at him. She meets his eyes, and sees something there she can't quite recognize. His eyes, his entire face, seem lit from within; he appears, for the first time, to be suffering from an emotion she can't read.

"Honey," she says, "what is it?"

He says, louder than necessary, "Mommy, I love you."

There is something odd in his voice, something chilling. It is a tone she's never heard from him before. He sounds frantic, foreign. He could be a refugee, someone with only rudimentary English, trying desperately to convey a need for which he has not learned the proper phrase.

"I love you too, baby," she replies, and although she's said the words thousands of times, she can hear the flanneled nervousness lodged now in her throat, the effort she must make to sound natural. She accelerates through the intersection. She drives carefully, with both hands precisely centered on the wheel.

It seems the boy will start crying again, as he does so often, so inexplicably, but his eyes remain bright and dry, unblinking.

"What's wrong?" she asks.

He continues staring at her. He does not blink.

He knows. He must know. The little boy can tell she's been somewhere illicit; he can tell she's lying. He watches her constantly, spends almost every waking hour in her presence. He's seen her with Kitty. He's watched her make a second cake, and bury the first one under other garbage in the can beside the garbage. He is devoted, entirely, to the observation and deciphering of her, because without her there is no world at all.

Of course he would know when she's lying.

She says, "Don't worry, honey. Everything's fine. We're going to have a wonderful party for Daddy's birthday tonight. Do you know how happy he'll be? We've got all these presents for him. We've made him such a nice cake."

Richie nods, unblinking. He rocks gently back and forth. Quietly, wishing to be overheard rather than heard, he says, "Yes, we've made him such a nice cake." There is a surprisingly mature hollowness in his voice.

He will watch her forever. He will always know when something is wrong. He will always know precisely when and how much she has failed.

"I love you, sweetheart," she says. "You're my guy." Briefly, for a moment, the boy changes shape. Briefly he glows, dead white. Laura remains not angry. She remembers to smile. She keeps both hands on the wheel.

Mrs. Dalloway

She has come to help Richard get ready for the party, but Richard does not respond to her knock. She knocks again, harder, then quickly, nervously, unlocks the door.

The apartment is full of light. Clarissa almost gasps at the threshold. All the shades have been raised, the windows opened. Although the air is filled only with the ordinary daylight that enters any tenement apartment on a sunny afternoon, it seems, in Richard's rooms, like a silent explosion. Here are his cardboard boxes, his bathtub (filthier than she'd realized), the dusty mirror and the expensive coffeemaker, all revealed in their true pathos, their ordinary smallness. It is, quite simply, the tenement apartment of a deranged person.

"Richard!" Clarissa calls.

"Mrs. Dalloway. Oh, Mrs. Dalloway, it's you."

She rushes into the other room and finds Richard still in his robe, perched on the sill of the open window, straddling it, with one emaciated leg still in the apartment and the other, invisible to her, dangling out over five stories.

"Richard," she says sternly. "Get down from there."

"It's so lovely out," he says. "What a day."

He looks insane and exalted, both ancient and childish, astride the windowsill like some scarecrow equestrian, a park statue by Giacometti. His hair is plastered to his scalp in some places, jutting out at sharp, rakish angles in others. His inside leg, bare to midthigh, blue-white, is skeletal but with a surprisingly solid little fist of calf muscle still clinging stubbornly to the bone.

"You're terrifying me," Clarissa says. "I want you to stop this and come inside. Now."

She moves toward him and he raises his inside leg to the sill. Only the heel of that foot, one hand, and one fleshless buttock remain in contact with the battered wood. On his robe, red-finned rockets emit perfect orange pinecones of fire. Helmeted astronauts, plump and white as the Uniroyal Man, faceless behind their dark visors, offer stiff, white-gloved salutes.

Richard says, "I took the Xanax *and* the Ritalin. They work wonderfully together. I feel wonderful. I opened all the blinds, but still, I found I wanted more air and light. I had a hard time getting up here, I don't mind telling you."

"Darling, please, put your leg back down on the floor. Will you do that for me?"

"I don't think I can make it to the party," he says. "I'm sorry."

"You don't have to. You don't have to do anything you don't want to do."

"What a day it is. What a beautiful, beautiful day."

Clarissa draws a breath, and another. She is surprisingly calm—she can feel herself acting well in a difficult situation—but at the same time is removed from herself, from the room, as if she is witnessing something that's already happened. It feels like a memory. Something within her, something like a voice but not a voice, an inner knowledge all but indistinguishable from the pump of her heart, says, *Once I found Richard sitting on a window ledge five stories above the ground.*

She says, "Get down from there. Please."

Richard's face darkens and contracts, as if Clarissa has posed him a difficult question. His empty chair, fully exposed in the daylight—leaking stuffing at its seams, the thin yellow towel on the seat embossed with rusty circles—could be the foolishness, the essential shoddiness, of mortal illness itself.

"Get *down* from there," Clarissa says. She speaks slowly and loudly, as if to a foreigner.

Richard nods, and does not move. His ravaged head, struck by full daylight, is geological. His flesh is as furrowed and pocked, as runneled, as desert stone.

He says, "I don't know if I can face this. You know. The party and the ceremony, and then the hour after that, and the hour after that."

"You don't have to go to the party. You don't have to go to the ceremony. You don't have to do anything at all."

"But there are still the hours, aren't there? One and then

another, and you get through that one and then, my god, there's another. I'm so sick."

"You have good days still. You know you do."

"Not really. It's kind of you to say so, but I've felt it for some time now, closing around me like the jaws of a gigantic flower. Isn't that a peculiar analogy? It feels that way, though. It has a certain vegetable inevitability. Think of the Venus flytrap. Think of kudzu choking a forest. It's a sort of juicy, green, thriving progress. Toward, well, you know. The green silence. Isn't it funny that, even now, it's difficult to say the word 'death'?"

"Are they here, Richard?"

"Who? Oh, the voices? The voices are always here."

"I mean, are you hearing them very distinctly?"

"No. I'm hearing you. It's always wonderful to hear you, Mrs. D. Do you mind that I still call you that?"

"Not at all. Come inside. Now."

"Remember her? Your alter ego? Whatever became of her?"

"This is her. I'm her. I need you to come inside. Will you, please?"

"It's so lovely here. I feel so free. Will you call my mother? She's all alone, you know."

"Richard—"

"Tell me a story, all right?"

"What kind of story?"

"Something from your day. From today. It could be the most ordinary thing. That would be better, actually. The most ordinary event you can think of."

"Richard—"

"Anything. Anything at all."

"Well, this morning, before I came here, I went to buy flowers for the party."

"Did you?"

"I did. It was a beautiful morning."

"Was it?"

"Yes. It was beautiful. It was so . . . fresh. I bought the flowers and took them home and put them in water. There. End of story. Now come inside."

"Fresh as if issued to children on a beach," Richard says.

"You could say that."

"Like a morning when we were young together."

"Yes. Like that."

"Like the morning you walked out of that old house, when you were eighteen and I was, well, I had just turned nineteen, hadn't I? I was a nineteen-year-old and I was in love with Louis and I was in love with you, and I thought I had never seen anything so beautiful as the sight of you walking out a glass door in the early morning, still sleepy, in your underwear. Isn't it strange?"

"Yes," Clarissa says. "Yes. It's strange."

"I've failed."

"Stop saying that. You haven't failed."

"I have. I'm not looking for sympathy. Not really. I just feel so sad. What I wanted to do seemed simple. I wanted to create something alive and shocking enough that it could stand beside a morning in somebody's life. The most ordinary morning. Imagine, trying to do that. What foolishness."

"It isn't the least bit foolish."

"I'm afraid I can't make the party."

"Please, please don't worry about the party. Don't think about the party. Give me your hand."

"You've been so good to me, Mrs. Dalloway."

"Richard—"

"I love you. Does that sound trite?"

"No."

Richard smiles. He shakes his head. He says, "I don't think two people could have been happier than we've been."

He inches forward, slides gently off the sill, and falls.

Clarissa screams, "No—"

He seems so certain, so serene, that she briefly imagines it hasn't happened at all. She reaches the window in time to see Richard still in flight, his robe billowing, and it seems even now as if it might be a minor accident, something reparable. She sees him touch the ground five floors below, sees him kneel on the concrete, sees his head strike, hears the sound he makes, and yet she believes, at least for another moment, leaning out over the sill, that he will stand up again, groggy perhaps, winded, but still himself, still whole, still able to speak.

She calls his name, once. It comes out as a question, far softer than she'd meant it to. He lies where he fell, face down, the robe thrown up over his head and his bare legs exposed, white against the dark concrete.

She runs from the room, out the door, which she leaves open behind her. She runs down the stairs. She thinks of calling for help, but doesn't. The air itself seems to have changed, to have come slightly apart; as if the atmosphere were palpably made of substance and its opposite. She runs down the stairs and is aware (she will be ashamed of this later) of herself as a woman running down a set of stairs, uninjured, still alive.

In the lobby she suffers through a moment of confusion over how to get to the air shaft where Richard lies, and she feels, briefly, as if she's gone to hell. Hell is a stale yellow box of a room, with no exit, shaded by an artificial tree, lined with scarred metal doors (one bears a Grateful Dead decal, a skull crowned with roses).

A door in the shadow of the stairwell, narrower than the others, leads outside, down a flight of broken cement stairs, to the place where Richard is. She knows even before she descends these last stairs that he is dead. His head is lost among the folds of the robe but she can see the puddle of blood, dark, almost black, that has formed where his head must be. She can see the utter stillness of his body, one arm extended at a peculiar angle, palm up, and both bare legs white and naked as death itself. He is still wearing the gray felt slippers she bought for him.

She descends these last stairs, sees that Richard is lying amid shards of broken glass, and takes a moment to realize it is simply the remains of a shattered beer bottle that had been lying on the concrete already, and not some consequence of Richard's fall. She thinks she must pick him up immediately, to get him off the glass.

She kneels beside him, puts a hand on his inert shoulder. Gently, very gently, as if she fears waking him, she pulls the robe down from around his head. All she can make sense of in the glistening mass of red, purple, and white are his parted lips and one open eye. She realizes she has made a sound, a sharp exclamation of surprise and pain. She covers his head again with the robe.

She remains kneeling at his side, uncertain about what to do next. She returns her hand to his shoulder. She does not stroke it; she simply rests her hand there. She tells herself she should go call the police, but doesn't want to leave Richard alone. She waits for someone to call down to her. She glances up at the ascending rows of windows, the hanging laundry, the perfect square of sky bisected by one thin blue-white blade of a cloud, and begins to understand that no one knows yet. No one has seen or heard Richard fall.

She does not move. She finds the window of the old woman, with its three ceramic statuettes (invisible from so far down). The old woman must be at home, she hardly ever goes out. Clarissa has an urge to shout up to her, as if she were some sort of family member; as if she should be informed. Clarissa puts off, at least for another minute or two, the inevitable next act. She remains with Richard, touching his shoulder. She feels (and is astonished at herself) slightly embarrassed by what has happened. She wonders why she doesn't weep. She is aware of the sound of her own breathing. She is aware of the slippers still on Richard's feet, of the sky reflected in the growing puddle of blood.

It ends here, then, on a pallet of concrete, under the clotheslines, amid shards of glass. She runs her hand, gently, down from his shoulder along the frail curve of his back. Guiltily, as if she is doing something forbidden, she leans over and rests her forehead against his spine while it is still, in some way, his; while he is still in some way Richard Worthington Brown. She can smell the stale flannel of the robe, the winey sharpness of his unbathed flesh. She would like to speak to him, but can't. She simply rests her head, lightly, against his back. If she were able to speak she would say something—she can't tell what, exactly—about how he has had the courage to create, and how, perhaps more important, he has had the courage to love singularly, over the decades, against all reason. She would talk to him about how she herself, Clarissa, loved him in return, loved him enormously, but left him on a street corner over thirty years ago (and, really, what else could she have done?). She would confess to her desire for a relatively ordinary life (neither more nor less than what most people desire), and to how much she wanted him to come to her party and exhibit his devotion in front of her guests. She would ask his forgiveness for shying away, on what would prove to be the day of his death, from kissing him on the lips, and for telling herself she did so only for the sake of his health.

Mrs. Brown

The candles are lit. The song is sung. Dan, blowing the candles out, sprays a few tiny droplets of clear spittle onto the icing's smooth surface. Laura applauds and, after a moment, Richie does, too.

"Happy birthday, darling," she says.

A spasm of fury rises unexpectedly, catches in her throat. He is coarse, gross, stupid; he has sprayed spit onto the cake. She herself is trapped here forever, posing as a wife. She must get through this night, and then tomorrow morning, and then another night here, in these rooms, with nowhere else to go. She must please; she must continue.

It might be like walking out into a field of brilliant snow. It could be dreadful and wonderful. *We thought her sorrows were ordinary sorrows; we had no idea.*

The anger passes. It's all right, she tells herself. It's all right. Pull yourself together, for heaven's sake.

Dan wraps his arm around her hips. Laura feels the meaty, scented solidity of him. She is sorry. She is aware, more than ever, of his goodness.

He says, "This is great. This is perfect."

She strokes the back of his head. His hair is slick with Vitalis, slightly coarse, like an otter's pelt. His face, stubbled now, has a sweaty shine, and his well-tended hair has relaxed enough to produce a single oily forelock, about the width of a blade of grass, that dangles to a point just above his brows. He has removed his tie, unbuttoned his shirt; he exudes a complex essence made up of sweat, Old Spice, the leather of his shoes, and the ineffable, profoundly familiar smell of his flesh—a smell with elements of iron, elements of bleach, and the remotest hint of cooking, as if deep inside him something moist and fatty were being fried.

Laura says to Richie, "Did you make a wish, too?"

He nods, though the possibility had not occurred to him. It seems he is always making a wish, every moment, and that his wishes, like his father's, have mainly to do with continuance. Like his father, what he wants most ardently is more of what he's already got (though, of course, if asked about the nature of his wishes, he would immediately rattle off a long list of toys, both actual and imaginary). Like his father he senses that more of this is precisely what they may very well not get.

"How would you like to help me cut the cake?" his father says.

"Yes," Richie answers.

Laura brings dessert plates and forks from the kitchen. Here she is, in this modest dining room, safe, with her husband and child, as Kitty lies in a hospital room waiting to hear what the doctors have found. Here they are, this family, in this place. All up and down their street, all up and down multitudes of streets, windows shine. Multitudes of dinners are served; the victories and setbacks of a multitude of days are narrated.

As Laura sets the plates and forks on the table—as they ring softly on the starched white cloth—it seems she has succeeded suddenly, at the last minute, the way a painter might brush a final line of color onto a painting and save it from incoherence; the way a writer might set down the line that brings to light the submerged patterns and symmetry in the drama. It has to do, somehow, with setting plates and forks on a white cloth. It is as unmistakable as it is unexpected.

Dan lets Richie remove the burnt-out candles before guiding his son's hands in slicing the cake. Laura watches. The dining room seems, right now, like the most perfect imaginable dining room, with its hunter-green walls and its dark maple hutch holding a trove of wedding silver. The room seems almost impossibly full: full of the lives of her husband and son; full of the future. It matters; it shines. Much of the world, whole countries, have been decimated, but a force that feels unambiguously like goodness has prevailed; even Kitty, it seems, will be healed by medical science. She will be healed. And if she's not, if she's past help, Dan and Laura and their son and the promise of the second child will all still be here, in this room, where a little boy frowns in concentration over the job of removing the candles and where his father holds one up to his mouth and exhorts him to lick off the frosting.

Laura reads the moment as it passes. Here it is, she thinks; there it goes. The page is about to turn.

She smiles at her son, serenely, from a distance. He smiles back. He licks the end of a burnt-out candle. He makes another wish.

Mrs. Woolf

She tries to concentrate on the book in her lap. Soon she and Leonard will leave Hogarth House and move to London. It has been decided. Virginia has won. She struggles to concentrate. The beef scraps have been scraped away, the table swept, the dishes washed.

She will go to the theater and concert halls. She will go to parties. She will haunt the streets, see everything, fill herself up with stories.

. . . life; London . . .

She will write and write. She will finish this book, then write another. She will remain sane and she will live as she was meant to live, richly and deeply, among others of her kind, in full possession and command of her gifts.

She thinks, suddenly, of Vanessa's kiss.

The kiss was innocent—innocent enough—but it was also

full of something not unlike what Virginia wants from London, from life; it was full of a love complex and ravenous, ancient, neither this nor that. It will serve as this afternoon's manifestation of the central mystery itself, the elusive brightness that shines from the edges of certain dreams; the brightness which, when we awaken, is already fading from our minds, and which we rise in the hope of finding, perhaps today, this new day in which anything might happen, anything at all. She, Virginia, has kissed her sister, not quite innocently, behind Nelly's broad, moody back, and now she is in a room with a book on her lap. She is a woman who will move to London.

Clarissa Dalloway will have loved a woman, yes; another woman, when she was young. She and the woman will have had a kiss, one kiss, like the singular enchanted kisses in fairy tales, and Clarissa will carry the memory of that kiss, the soaring hope of it, all her life. She will never find a love like that which the lone kiss seemed to offer.

Virginia, excited, rises from her chair and puts her book on the table. Leonard asks from his own chair, "Are you going to bed?"

"No. It's early, isn't it?"

He scowls at his watch. "It's nearly half past ten," he says.

"I'm just restless. I'm not tired yet."

"I'd like you to go to bed at eleven," he says.

She nods. She will remain on good behavior, now that London's been decided on. She leaves the parlor, crosses the hall, and enters the darkened dining room. Long rectangles of moonlight mixed with street light fall through the window onto the tabletop, are swept away by windblown branches, reappear, and are swept away again. Virginia stands in the doorway, watching the shifting patterns as she would watch waves break on a beach. Yes, Clarissa will have loved a woman. Clarissa will have kissed a woman, only once. Clarissa will be bereaved, deeply lonely, but she will not die. She will be too much in love with life, with London. Virginia imagines someone else, yes, someone strong of body but frail-minded; someone with a touch of genius, of poetry, ground under by the wheels of the world, by war and government, by doctors; a someone who is, technically speaking, insane, because that person sees meaning everywhere, knows that trees are sentient beings and sparrows sing in Greek. Yes, someone like that. Clarissa, sane Clarissa—exultant, ordinary Clarissa—will go on, loving London, loving her life of ordinary pleasures, and someone else, a deranged poet, a visionary, will be the one to die.

Mrs. Brown

She finishes brushing her teeth. The dishes have been washed and put away, Richie is in bed, her husband is waiting. She rinses the brush under the tap, rinses her mouth, spits into the sink. Her husband will be on his side of the bed, looking up at the ceiling with his hands clasped behind his head. When she enters the room he will look at her as if he is surprised and happy to see her here, his wife, of all people, about to remove her robe, drape it over the chair, and climb into bed with him. That is his way—boyish surprise; a suave, slightly abashed glee; a deep and distracted innocence with sex coiled inside like a spring. She thinks sometimes, can't help thinking, of those cans of peanuts sold in novelty shops, the ones with the paper snakes waiting to pop out when the lids are opened. There will be no reading tonight.

She slips her toothbrush back into its slot in the porcelain holder.

When she looks in the medicine-cabinet mirror, she briefly imagines that someone is standing behind her. There is no one, of course; it's just a trick of the light. For an instant, no more than that, she has imagined some sort of ghost self, a second version of her, standing immediately behind, watching. It's nothing. She opens the medicine cabinet, puts the toothpaste away. Here, on the glass shelves, are the various lotions and sprays, the bandages and ointments, the medicines. Here is the plastic prescription bottle with its sleeping pills. This bottle, the most recent refill, is almost full—she can't use them, of course, while she's pregnant.

She takes the bottle off the shelf, holds it up to the light. There are at least thirty pills inside, maybe more. She puts it back on the shelf.

It would be as simple as checking into a hotel room. It would be as simple as that. Think how wonderful it might be to no longer matter. Think how wonderful it might be to no longer worry, or struggle, or fail.

What if that moment at dinner—that equipoise, that small perfection—were enough? What if you decided to want no more?

She closes the medicine-cabinet door, which meets the frame with a solid, competent metallic click. She thinks of everything inside the cabinet, on the shelves, in darkness now. She goes into the bedroom, where her husband is waiting. She removes her robe.

"Hi," he says confidently, tenderly, from his side of the bed.

"Did you have a nice birthday?" she asks.

"The greatest." He pulls back the sheet for her but she hesitates, standing at the side of the bed, wearing her filmy blue nightgown. She can't seem to feel her body, though she knows it's there.

"That's good," she says. "I'm glad you had a nice time."

"You coming to bed?" he says.

"Yes," she answers, and does not move. She might, at this moment, be nothing but a floating intelligence; not even a brain inside a skull, just a presence that perceives, as a ghost might. Yes, she thinks, this is probably how it must feel to be a ghost. It's a little like reading, isn't it—that same sensation of knowing people, settings, situations, without playing any particular part beyond that of the willing observer.

"So," Dan says after a while. "Are you coming to bed?"

"Yes," she says.

From far away, she can hear a dog barking.

Mrs. Dalloway

Clarissa puts her hand on the old woman's shoulder, as if to prepare her for some further shock. Sally, who has preceded them down the hallway, opens the door.

"Here we are," Clarissa says.

"Yes," Laura replies.

When they enter the apartment, Clarissa is relieved to see that Julia has put away the hors d'oeuvres. The flowers, of course, remain—brilliant and innocent, exploding from vases in lavish, random profusion, for Clarissa dislikes arrangements. She prefers flowers to look as if they've just arrived, in armloads, from the fields.

Beside a vase full of roses, Julia sleeps on the sofa with a book open on her lap. In sleep she sits with an air of surprising dignity, even authority, foursquare, shoulders relaxed and both feet on the floor, head bowed discreetly forward, as if in prayer.

At this moment she could be a minor goddess come to attend to mortal anxiety; come to sit with grave, loving certainty and whisper, from her trance, to those who enter, It's all right, don't be frightened, all you have to do is die.

"We're back," Sally says.

Julia wakes, blinks, and rises. The spell is broken; Julia is a girl again. Sally strides into the room, shrugging off her jacket as she walks, and there is a brief impression of Clarissa and the old woman standing shyly in a vestibule, hanging back, carefully removing their gloves, though there is no vestibule and they are not wearing gloves.

Clarissa says, "Julia, this is Laura Brown."

Julia steps forward, stops at a respectful distance from Laura and Clarissa. Where did she get such poise and presence, Clarissa wonders. She's still a girl.

"I'm so sorry," Julia says.

Laura says, "Thank you," in a clearer, firmer voice than Clarissa had expected from her.

Laura is a tall, slightly stooped woman of eighty or more. Her hair is a bright, steely gray; her skin is translucent, parchment-colored, aswarm with brown freckles the size of pinpricks. She wears a dark floral dress and soft, crepey, old-woman shoes.

Clarissa urges her forward, into the room. A silence passes. Out of the silence rises a feeling that Clarissa, Sally, and even Laura have arrived, nervous and edgy, knowing no one, more than a little underdressed, at a party being given by Julia.

"Thanks for cleaning up, Julie," Sally says.

"I reached almost everyone on the list," Julia says. "A few people showed up. Louis Waters."

"Oh, god. He didn't get my message."

"And there were two women, I don't remember their names. And somebody else, a black man, Gerry something."

"Gerry Jarman," Clarissa says. "Was it pretty awful?"

"Gerry Jarman was all right. Louis sort of, well, broke down. He stayed almost an hour. I had a long talk with him. He seemed better when he left. Sort of better."

"I'm sorry, Julia. I'm sorry you had to handle all this."

"It was fine. Please don't worry about me."

Clarissa nods. She says to Laura, "You must be exhausted."

"I'm not quite sure what I am," Laura says.

"Please sit down," Clarissa says. "Do you think you could eat something?"

"Oh, I don't believe so. Thank you."

Clarissa guides Laura to the sofa. Laura sits gratefully but cautiously, as if she were very tired but could not be certain the sofa was entirely stable.

Julia comes and stands before Laura, leans close to her ear.

"I'm going to make you a cup of tea," she says. "Or there's coffee. Or a brandy."

"A cup of tea would be nice. Thank you."

"You really *should* eat something, too," Julia says. "I'll bet you haven't eaten since you left home, have you?"

"Well—"

Julia says, "I'm just going to put a few things out in the kitchen."

"That's very nice, dear," Laura says.

Julia glances at Clarissa. "Mother," she says, "you stay here with Mrs. Brown. Sally and I will go see what we've got."

"Fine," Clarissa says. She sits beside Laura on the sofa. She simply does what her daughter tells her to, and finds a surprising relief in it. Maybe, she thinks, one could begin dying into this: the ministrations of a grown daughter, the comforts of a room. Here, then, is age. Here are the little consolations, the lamp and the book. Here is the world, increasingly managed by people who are not you; who will do either well or badly; who do not look at you when they pass you in the street.

Sally says to Clarissa, "Does it seem too morbid to eat the food from the party? It's all still here."

"I don't think so," Clarissa says. "I think Richard would probably have appreciated that."

She looks nervously at Laura. Laura smiles, hugs her elbows, seems to see something on the toes of her shoes.

"Yes," Laura says. "I think he would, indeed."

"Okay, then," Sally says. She and Julia go into the kitchen.

According to the clock, it is ten minutes past midnight. Laura sits with a certain prim self-containment, lips pressed together, eyes half closed. She is, Clarissa thinks, just waiting for this hour to end. She is waiting until she can be in bed, alone.

Clarissa says, "You can go right to bed if you'd like to, Laura. The guest room's just down the hall."

"Thank you," Laura says. "I will, in a little while."

They settle into another silence, one that is neither intimate nor particularly uncomfortable. Here she is, then, Clarissa thinks; here is the woman from Richard's poetry. Here is the lost mother, the thwarted suicide; here is the woman who walked away. It is both shocking and comforting that such a figure could, in fact, prove to be an ordinary-looking old woman seated on a sofa with her hands in her lap.

Clarissa says, "Richard was a wonderful man."

She regrets it instantly. Already, the doomed little eulogies begin; already someone who's died is reassessed as a respectable citizen, a doer of good deeds, a wonderful man. Why did she say such a thing? To console an old woman, really, and to ingratiate herself. And, all right, she said it to stake her claim on the body: *I knew him most intimately, I am the one who'll be first to take his measure.* She would like, at this moment, to order Laura Brown to go to bed, shut the door, and stay in her room until morning.

"Yes," Laura says. "And he was a wonderful writer, wasn't he?"

"You've read the poems?"

"I have. And the novel."

She knows, then. She knows all about Clarissa, and she knows that she herself, Laura Brown, is the ghost and goddess in a small body of private myths made public (if "public" isn't a term too grand for the small, stubborn band of poetry readers who remain). She knows she has been worshipped and despised; she knows she has obsessed a man who might, conceivably, prove to be a significant artist. Here she sits, freckled, in a floral print dress. She says calmly, of her son, that he was a wonderful writer.

"Yes," Clarissa says helplessly. "He was a wonderful writer." What else can she say?

"You were never his editor, were you?"

"No. We were too close. It would have been too complicated."

"Yes. I understand."

"Editors need a certain objectivity."

"Of course they do."

Clarissa feels as if she's suffocating. How can this be so difficult? Why is it so impossible to speak plainly to Laura Brown, to ask the important questions? What *are* the important questions?

Clarissa says, "I took the best care of him I could."

Laura nods. She says, "I wish I could have done better."

"I wish the same thing myself."

Laura reaches over and takes Clarissa's hand. Under the soft, loose skin of Laura's hand, palpably, are the spines and knobs of bones, the cords of veins.

Laura says, "We did the best we could, dear. That's all anyone can do, isn't it?"

"Yes, it is," Clarissa says.

So Laura Brown, the woman who tried to die and failed at it, the woman who fled her family, is alive when all the others, all those who struggled to survive in her wake, have passed away. She is alive now, after her ex-husband has been carried off by liver cancer, after her daughter has been killed by a drunk driver. She is alive after Richard has jumped from a window onto a bed of broken glass.

Clarissa holds the old woman's hand. What else can she do?

Clarissa says, "I wonder if Julia has remembered your tea."

"I'm sure she has, dear."

Clarissa glances over at the glass doors that lead to the modest garden. She and Laura Brown are reflected, imperfectly, in the black glass. Clarissa thinks of Richard on the windowsill; Richard letting go; not jumping, really, but sliding as if from a rock into water. What must it have been like, the moment he had irrevocably done it; the moment he was out of his dark apartment and released into air? What must it have been like to see the alley below, with its blue and brown garbage cans, its spray of amber glass, come rushing up? Was it—could it possibly have been—a pleasure of some kind to crumple onto the pavement and feel (did he momentarily feel?) the skull crack open, all its impulses, its little lights, spilled out? There can't, Clarissa thinks, have been much pain. There would have been the idea of pain, its first shock, and then—whatever came next.

"I'm going to go see," she says to Laura. "I'll be back in a minute."

"All right," Laura says.

Clarissa stands, a bit unsteadily, and goes into the kitchen. Sally and Julia have taken the food from the refrigerator and piled it on the counters. There are spirals of grilled chicken breast, flecked black, touched with brilliant yellow, impaled on wooden picks, arranged around a bowl of peanut sauce. There are miniature onion tarts. There are steamed shrimp, and glistening bright-red squares of rare tuna with dabs of wasabi. There are dark triangles of grilled eggplant, and round sandwiches on brown bread, and endive leaves touched at their stem ends with discrete smears of goat cheese and chopped walnuts. There are shallow bowls full of raw vegetables. And there is, in its earthenware dish, the crab casserole Clarissa made herself, for Richard, because it was his favorite.

"My god," Clarissa says. "Look at all this."

"We were expecting fifty people," Sally says.

They stand for a moment, the three of them, before the plates heaped with food. The food feels pristine, untouchable; it could be a display of relics. It seems, briefly, to Clarissa, that the food—that most perishable of entities—will remain here after she and the others have disappeared; after all of them, even Julia, have died. Clarissa imagines the food still here, still fresh somehow, untouched, as she and the others leave these rooms, one by one, forever.

Sally takes Clarissa's head in her hands. She kisses Clarissa's forehead firmly and competently, in a way that reminds Clarissa of putting a stamp on a letter.

"Let's feed everybody and go to bed," she says softly, close to Clarissa's ear. "It's time for this day to be over."

Clarissa squeezes Sally's shoulder. She would say, "I love you," but of course Sally knows. Sally returns the pressure on Clarissa's upper arm.

"Yes," Clarissa says. "It's time."

It seems, at that moment, that Richard begins truly to leave the world. To Clarissa it is an almost physical sensation, a gentle but irreversible pulling-away, like a blade of grass being drawn out of the ground. Soon Clarissa will sleep, soon everyone who knew him will be asleep, and they'll all wake up tomorrow morning to find that he's joined the realm of the dead. She wonders if tomorrow morning will mark not only the end of Richard's earthly life but the beginning of the end of his poetry, too. There are, after all, so many books. Some of them, a handful, are good, and of that handful, only a few survive. It's possible that the citizens of the future, people not yet born, will want to read Richard's elegies, his beautifully cadenced laments, his rigorously unsentimental offerings of love and fury, but it's far more likely that his books will vanish along with almost everything else. Clarissa, the figure in a novel, will vanish, as will Laura Brown, the lost mother, the martyr and fiend.

Yes, Clarissa thinks, it's time for the day to be over. We throw our parties; we abandon our families to live alone in Canada; we struggle to write books that do not change the world, despite our gifts and our unstinting efforts, our most extravagant hopes. We live our lives, do whatever we do, and then we sleep—it's as simple and ordinary as that. A few jump out of windows or drown themselves or take pills; more die by accident; and most of us, the vast majority, are slowly devoured by some disease or, if we're very fortunate, by time itself. There's just this for consolation: an hour here or there when our lives seem, against all odds and expectations, to burst open and give us everything we've ever imagined, though everyone but children (and perhaps even they) knows these hours will inevitably be followed by others, far darker and more difficult. Still, we cherish the city, the morning; we hope, more than anything, for more.

Heaven only knows why we love it so.

Here, then, is the party, still laid; here are the flowers, still fresh; everything ready for the guests, who have turned out to be only four. Forgive us, Richard. It is, in fact, a party, after all. It is a party for the not-yet-dead; for the relatively undamaged; for those who for mysterious reasons have the fortune to be alive.

It is, in fact, great good fortune.

Julia says, "Do you think I should make a plate for Richard's mother?"

"No," Clarissa says. "I'll go get her."

She returns to the living room, to Laura Brown. Laura smiles wanly at Clarissa—who could possibly know what she thinks or feels? Here she is, then; the woman of wrath and sorrow, of pathos, of dazzling charm; the woman in love with death; the victim and torturer who haunted Richard's work. Here, right here in this room, is the beloved; the traitor. Here is an old woman, a retired librarian from Toronto, wearing old woman's shoes.

And here she is, herself, Clarissa, not Mrs. Dalloway anymore; there is no one now to call her that. Here she is with another hour before her.

"Come in, Mrs. Brown," she says. "Everything's ready."

Acknowledgments

I was helped enormously in the revising of this book by Jill Ciment, Judy Clain, Joel Conarroe, Stacey D'Erasmo, Bonnie Friedman, Marie Howe, and Adam Moss. Research, technical advice, and other forms of aid were generously provided by Dennis Dermody, Paul Elie, Carmen Gomezplata, Bill Hamilton, Ladd Spiegel, John Waters, and Wendy Welker. My agent, Gail Hochman, and my editor, Jonathan Galassi, are secular saints. Tracy O'Dwyer and Patrick Giles have provided more in the way of general inspiration than they may know, by reading as widely, discerningly, and voluptuously as they do. My parents and sister are great readers too, though that does not begin to account for their contributions. Donna Lee and Cristina Thorson remain essential in more ways than I can enumerate here.

Three Lives and Company, a bookstore owned and operated

by Jill Dunbar and Jenny Feder, is a sanctuary and, to me, the center of the civilized universe. It has for some time been the most reliable place to go when I need to remember why novels are still worth the trouble they take to write.

I received a residency from the Engelhard Foundation and a grant from the Mrs. Giles Whiting Foundation, both of which mattered considerably.

I am deeply grateful to all.

A Note on Sources

While Virginia Woolf, Leonard Woolf, Vanessa Bell, Nelly Boxall, and other people who actually lived appear in this book as fictional characters, I have tried to render as accurately as possible the outward particulars of their lives as they would have been on a day I've invented for them in 1923. I depended for information on a number of sources, most prominently two magnificently balanced and insightful biographies: *Virginia Woolf: A Biography* by Quentin Bell, and *Virginia Woolf* by Hermione Lee. Also essential were *Virginia Woolf: The Impact of Childhood Sexual Abuse on Her Life and Work* by Louise de Salvo, *Virginia Woolf* by James King, *Selected Letters of Vanessa Bell* edited by Regina Marler, *Woman of Letters: A Life of Virginia Woolf* by Phyllis Rose, *A Marriage of True Minds: An Intimate Portrait of Leonard and Virginia Woolf* by George Spater and Ian Parsons, and *Beginning Again: An Autobiography of the*

Years 1911 to 1918 and *Downhill All the Way: An Autobiography of the Years 1919 to 1939*, by Leonard Woolf. A chapter on *Mrs. Dalloway* in Joseph Boone's book *Libidinal Currents: Sexuality and the Shaping of Modernism* was illuminating, as was an article by Janet Malcolm, "A House of One's Own," which appeared in *The New Yorker* in 1995. I also learned a great deal from the introductions to various editions of *Mrs. Dalloway*: Maureen Howard's in the Harcourt Brace & Co. edition, Elaine Showalter's in the Penguin, and Claire Tomalin's in the Oxford. I am indebted to Anne Olivier Bell for collecting and editing Woolf's diaries, to Andrew McNeillie for assisting her, and to Nigel Nicolson and Joanne Trautmann for collecting and editing Woolf's letters. When I visited Monk's House in Rodmell, Joan Jones was gracious and informative. To all these people, I offer my thanks.